β

A Dead Liberty

A Dead Liberty

CATHERINE AIRD, pseud.

PUBLISHED FOR THE CRIME CLUB BY

DOUBLEDAY & COMPANY, INC.

GARDEN CITY, NEW YORK

1987

The chapter headings are taken from the
old British National Formulary.

Library of Congress Cataloging-in-Publication Data

Aird, Catherine, pseud.
A dead liberty.

I. Title.
PR6051.I65D4   1987   823'.914   86-16753
ISBN 0-385-23554-2

for North, South, East and West
—with love

Acknowledgement
B. R. Rafferty—*notaire*

A Dead Liberty

ONE

Guttae Pro Oculis—Eye drops

"Come along now," said the Chairman of the Bench briskly. "This isn't getting us anywhere, you know."

The girl standing before him made no reply whatsoever.

"You heard what the Clerk said," went on Henry Simmonds, not unkindly. He knew that a first appearance in the dock of a Magistrates' Court was a daunting business for anyone, and this girl was quite young. And, as far as he could judge after casting his practised eye over the courtroom for obvious friends and relatives, she was also quite alone.

"I'll ask the Clerk to repeat the charge," said Mr. Simmonds when the girl made no reply, "in case you didn't hear it properly."

The Clerk to the Berebury Magistrates' Court heroically refrained from raising his voice as he repeated himself for the third time. In a manner that befitted his long years on the administrative side of the law, he also kept any unnecessary inflexion out of his tone. The words themselves were in any case quite awe-inspiring enough as it was.

He said again "Lucy Mirabel Durmast, you are charged that on or about the thirteenth of January last you did feloniously cause the death of Kenneth Malcolm Carline against the Peace of Our Sovereign Lady the Queen, her Crown and Dignity . . ."

There was a full-size Royal Coat of Arms of Her Majesty Queen Elizabeth II affixed to the wall of the court at a level above and behind the Chairman's head. If the girl in the dock thought it odd that the act of murder should still be seen—even in this conspicuously egalitarian day and age—as a breach of the Queen's Peace, she did not say so. She raised her head and gravely regarded the Clerk of the Court with bright grey-green eyes, but she did not utter a single word.

The Chairman of the Bench shuffled his papers and took the opportunity while the charge was being read again of having a good look at the person standing before him. She looked about twenty years old, but she could have been more. As his wife constantly reminded him, he was apt to underestimate women's ages. Although Mrs. Simmonds gracefully conceded this to be a good fault in a husband, it wasn't a help on the Bench. If she were under eighteen, he mused to himself, she was *doli capax*, which as the Clerk was sure to remind him at the earliest opportunity, meant she was capable of committing a crime but not always liable to be punished for so doing in the same way as someone of eighteen and older.

Time was when a man could tell a girl's age from her clothes but not any more. This girl—actually she hadn't even admitted to being Lucy Mirabel Durmast either yet, but Henry Simmonds had no reason to suppose she wasn't—was dressed rather more carefully than most of those who appeared before him but not in a way that told him very much about her. She had on a plain velvet jacket in a shade of mid-brown that went very well with her shoulder-length hair, which was of a dark shade of auburn. Beneath the velvet jacket she was wearing a pale, lemon-coloured blouse. Below them both Henry Simmonds was fairly confident that she would be wearing a patterned pleated skirt but the height of the dock prevented him from seeing this for himself.

Over his long years as a lay magistrate Henry Simmonds had schooled himself not to associate sartorial appearance of any sort with either guilt or innocence—but that did not mean he didn't notice clothes. In his day all manner of styles and degrees of fashion had come before him. He had, for instance, been aware rather more quickly than most when the ethnic look had been overtaken by its successor—but he had learned long ago not to be too influenced by them. Guilt, he knew, did not necessarily go with unkempt clothes or a dirty appearance—or indeed with dirt itself—although he was well aware that without exception all the solicitors in Berebury advised their clients that a neat and tidy look went down well with the magistrates.

And short hair.

Actually Henry Simmonds was always a little wary of a short back-and-sides hair cut that had a freshly barbered look about it, but he never said so—not even to his fellow magistrates. And he was noticeably less affected by long, straggling locks and a beard on a young man than the rest of the Bench with whom he sat. They were apt to bracket having long hair with the charge and to think of it as another and separate offence.

The girl in the dock had lovely hair. It fell down on her shoulders with an entirely natural grace.

Even when the members of the Bench were in the privacy of their retiring room discussing sentences and the other magistrates muttered something about "and get his hair cut" as if it were either an additional punishment or a remedy for ill-doing, Henry Simmonds always resisted the temptation to join in. This was entirely due to the influence of his great-aunts. He was old enough to remember their finding a new young medical assistant to their old family doctor unacceptable because he was clean-shaven—but then, they had been brought up in the era of the grand beard that had only gradually given way to the mutton chop and the sideburn.

"Do you wish to say anything?" asked the Clerk to the the Magistrates.

Lucy Durmast turned her head attentively in his direction but made no reply.

Henry Simmonds was still thinking about her clothes.

It was quite difficult, he conceded silently to himself, for anyone to know the correct garment to wear for an appearance in Court but this girl had clearly applied her mind to the problem. There was nothing in the least bit way out in what she had on, but nothing apologetic either. She had seen to it that someone had brought in suitable garments for her to wear and she was as well groomed as prison facilities allowed.

"Have you anything to say?" The Clerk let a note of peremptoriness creep into his voice. "Do you wish to bring witnesses?"

The peremptory note did not affect Lucy Durmast's resolution —if that was what it was—not to speak, and she did not answer him.

There was that though about the way in which she held her head high and yet courteously inclined that made Henry Simmonds reflect that in an earlier day and age Lucy Durmast might have dressed for a different sort of Court appearance. Presentation there in that other Court—a vague memory of old sepia-coloured photographs floated through his mind—meant that you were being brought to the Sovereign's attention in a different way.

And yet, in a curious fashion, both Courts were the Sovereign's houses—that was what the very word "Court" meant. The Court was the place where the King or Queen was. The fact that he, Henry Simmonds of Almstone, Justice of the Peace, was there to-day in the Court at Berebury as the Queen's surrogate descended directly from the fact that Her Majesty couldn't be in every Court up and down the land at the same time—while Justice demanded that she should be. In essence Henry Simmonds of Almstone held the Queen's Commission to act on her behalf.

"Do you wish to say anything?" said the Clerk again.

Answer came there none.

There was not even, noted Henry Simmonds, the faintest shake or nod of that fine head of hair that could possibly be construed as a response to the most dreadful charge in the book. The girl held herself quite still, almost as if she were afraid that any movement at all might be taken for what it was not.

And erect, too.

There was nothing cringing about her posture. No one could have implied guilt from anything about the way in which she stood.

The Clerk fell back on a more ancient formula still. "Lucy Mirabel Durmast, how say you?"

Lucy Mirabel Durmast said nothing at all.

Henry Simmonds wondered if anyone had ever told Lucy Durmast how beautiful her hair was. He glanced down at the list of cases on the bench in front of him to remind himself of a name: Kenneth Malcolm Carline. Had Kenneth Carline ever said anything about Lucy Durmast's hair, he wondered?

Before he was murdered, that is.

If he had been murdered, of course.

The Clerk put down his paper and looked straight at the girl in the dock.

She returned his gaze thoughtfully but said nothing.

There was a stage of response to a situation, Henry Simmonds reminded himself, that was known as "a bit late back." It was meant to demonstrate that due consideration had been given to the subject under discussion. As the moments of silence ticked by, it was borne in upon him that this was an eventuality that did not apply in this case. He realised that Lucy Durmast was not simply playing for time. She was clearly not going to speak at all.

Henry Simmonds felt a stirring at his side and was reminded by it that the very word Bench was a noun of multitude. He was not sitting alone today although he might have been. He was flanked by two fellow magistrates, both of whom were no doubt thankful that the honour of the Chair was resting on his manly shoulders rather than theirs.

Actually not all their shoulders were manly. Mrs. Mabel Sperry presented the outward picture of the archetypal wife and mother in spite of having a sentencing policy on the Judge Jeffery's side of severe. The third member of the Bench today was young and politically ambitious. He had still to blunt his armour on the realities of the Magistrates' Court. Terry Watkins, appointed by the Lord Chancellor's Office to keep a social balance in Middle England, saw himself as representing Common Man and usually spoke accordingly. So far he had been unusually silent, which meant that he felt there was no underdog to be spoken up for. Henry Simmonds concurred with this unexpressed view. Young and alone as she was, Lucy Durmast did not give the impression of belonging to an oppressed minority.

It must then have been Mrs. Sperry who had made a movement. She was doubtless itching to remind him that no reply to a charge constituted a technical plea of Not Guilty. But he was in no hurry to proceed. Henry Simmonds was a humane man, more than competent and well aware what was required of him by the peculiar triumvirate made up of the Lord Chancellor's Office, the great British Public and—oddly enough—those arraigned before him for misdemeanours arising out of various degrees of deviance from the Common Law.

There was a Fourth Estate, too, only it was never mentioned.

Henry Simmonds hadn't realised this until he had been on the Bench a little while. He wouldn't have wanted to admit it for worlds, but he was aware that the expectations of the police force came into the matter too. It had been some time before he had appreciated that improperly light sentences almost always resulted in the speedy reappearance of the offender before the Bench on another charge.

In the ordinary way he picked his way through the minefield of everybody's conception of justice with a sure touch, but today was rather different. Henry Simmonds had his normal share of human curiosity too. He was more than a little intrigued by the girl before him as well as by her silence.

For one thing she patently didn't fit the usual run of petty offenders who came the way of the Berebury Bench and he couldn't remember when he had last seen anyone facing a charge of murder who was young and pretty and female. Lucy Durmast certainly didn't fit the usual run of homicidal criminals whom he had seen either. Most murderers, his police friends were wont to say with a touch of cynicism, are male and—as a rule—widowers by the time they appeared in Court.

"Have you heard the indictment?" he asked the girl himself. If she were deaf, the newspapers would enjoy themselves at his expense on Friday.

She turned her head from the Magistrates' Clerk towards him as he spoke, so she had heard it all right, but she still did not speak. At least she was facing him, he thought philosophically. There were those who demonstrated that they did not recognise the jurisdiction of the Court by turning their backs on those sitting in judgement.

"And do you understand it?" asked Henry Simmonds mildly.

There had been a memorable motoring case in his Court once when an interpreter had had to be sent for on behalf of a Bulgarian driver whose English had been limited to "please" and "thank you." Vitally important as Henry Simmonds's nanny had always insisted these two phrases were, they hadn't got the man very far in defending a charge of driving a motor vehicle without due care and attention.

Unfortunately the interpreter's Bulgarian had been better than his knowledge of the law and he had enthusiastically entered the lists in defence of the erring motorist. Whoever had said that only a Bishop gained by translation was right. Without the detached impartiality of the true translator, the case had fallen . . .

"Charge." Henry Simmonds's train of thought was interrupted by a whisper from the Clerk to the Magistrates. "Not indictment."

"What was that?" he asked, sotto voce.

"Charge, Mr. Simmonds," insisted the Clerk. "Not indictment. She's here on a charge."

He nodded and turned courteously to the prisoner. "The Clerk has quite properly reminded me that you come before this Court on a charge and not on an indictment."

The Bench was entitled to believe that Lucy Durmast had been advised on the difference between the two and knew what an indictment was. If she did know, thought Henry Simmonds, then she was a better man than he was. He certainly hadn't grasped the detail at his own first appearance on the Bench. All he'd had at the back of his mind then had been something called "a True Bill," which he had read about somewhere, but that, he had been told at the time, was an archaism that had been left behind in some reform or other.

"An indictment," he explained now as there was no visible sign of anyone acting for the Defense," is a written accusation made on behalf of the Sovereign . . ."

There was the Queen cropping up again.

This time Lucy Durmast's gaze did tilt fractionally upwards to take in the Royal Coat of Arms above his head. Henry Simmonds wondered if she knew what the motto on the scroll beneath the crest meant—*Honi Soit qui mal y pense.* He always thought it very apposite for a Court of Law—Evil unto him who evil thinks. And not written in Latin either but in Norman French. Perhaps it had come over with William the Conqueror, or was it merely a legacy of those days when England's territory rather than her tourists had extended into France?

It was a visit to the Abbey at Fontevrault that had cemented that period of history in Henry Simmonds's mind. It hadn't been so much the royal tombs themselves lying there in the transept— Henry II and his wife, Eleanor of Aquitaine, Richard Lionheart and Isabelle of Angoulême—as the fact that the French Government wouldn't even now let the Foreign Office arrange for them to come back to lie at Windsor that had underscored the past to him.

"An indictment . . ." He wouldn't be at all surprised to learn that that word had come over with William the Conqueror too. That might explain why it wasn't pronounced as it was spelt.

"An indictment," he persisted, "sets out a serious crime . . ." He paused and decided that to explain that murder was a serious crime would be mere pedantry.

And yet, oddly enough, the only time when he had fallen into argument with Terry Watkins had been over the age-old allegation that the Bench always felt more strongly about the defence of property than it did about attacks on the person. Goodness knew who would have been the first malcontent to say that—a disgruntled peasant in the Middle Ages probably. It was certainly old hat by Wat Tyler's day.

The young radical Watkins had once quoted Proudhon's dictum "Property is theft" to the others in the Magistrates' Retiring Room. This hadn't gone down very well with Mrs. Mabel Sperry. To begin with, she hadn't understood what Terry Watkins had been talking about, and when it did eventually dawn on her she hadn't liked what he had said.

Henry Simmonds would have liked at that point to have brought in a mention of Victor Hugo's piece from *Les Misérables* about the Bishop's candlesticks—countering one Frenchman with another rather neatly, he thought—but Terry Watkins and Mrs. Sperry had fallen into such bitter argument that he had had practically to bind the pair of them over to keep the peace under one of the oldest statutes in the book.

In their own recognizances, too.

He cleared his throat, looked at Lucy Durmast and finished his piece from the chair ". . . for which the accused may be tried by jury."

Lucy Durmast still did not speak but she did turn her head to look at the jury box.

It was empty.

She looked back at Henry Simmonds. For one fleeting moment he thought she might also have raised her eyebrows slightly too, but he could have been mistaken in this. Silent she might be, unresponsive she was most certainly not.

"This is not a trial." Henry Simmonds seized upon the opening that this created—if such it could be called. It certainly wasn't a dialogue because Lucy Durmast still hadn't spoken. Non-verbal communication described what had happened better.

This time Lucy Durmast's gaze drifted in the direction of the prosecuting solicitor representing the Director of Public Prosecution. There was nobody sitting beside him on behalf of the Defence. Henry Simmonds always thought how subtle it was that those acting for the Prosecution and the Defence should sit side by side in Court. This was because they weren't supposed to be surrogate adversaries in the tournament sense but—in theory at least—

both servants of that mythical and abstract concept known as Justice.

"These are only committal proceedings," said Henry firmly. This was one of the reasons why he wasn't too worried that Lucy Durmast hadn't replied to the charge. Time was when a prisoner couldn't plead guilty to a charge of murder anyway. That was the Law bending over backwards to see that no one went to the gallows without a fair trial.

He amplified this, too, lest there be any misunderstanding. "Committal proceedings are short dress rehearsals of the prosecution case, so to speak, to give the defence a chance to know what case it must answer."

Lucy Durmast ran her tongue over lips that looked as if they had gone suddenly dry but she used neither tongue nor lips for speech.

"And," went on Henry Simmonds formally, "to enable the magistrates to decide whether a jury, acting reasonably, could convict on such evidence and thus whether to commit the case for full trial at a higher Court."

In the event, after they had heard the evidence the Examining Justices didn't even retire . . .

TWO

Linimenta—Liniments

"Not a word?" barked Superintendent Leeyes incredulously. His office in Berebury Police Station was only little more than a stone's throw from the Magistrates' Court.

"Not a word, sir," replied Detective Inspector Sloan, who had arrived back there hotfoot from the Court.

"Are you sure, Sloan?"

"Not a single dicky bird," declared Detective Inspector Sloan with all the assurance of someone who had been there.

"All day?" said Leeyes irascibly. "Do you mean to tell me that that girl didn't say a thing all day?"

"All day," intoned Sloan.

"It would have to happen to us," complained Leeyes. He was inclined to self-pity anyway and a totally silent prisoner could only mean trouble: there was no doubt about that.

"Yes, sir."

"The last thing we needed, of course, was a difficult woman."

"Yes, sir," agreed Inspector Sloan with something approaching fervour.

"The last thing any setup needs is a difficult woman." He grunted. "They've got one on the Watch Committee, too, Sloan, and . . ."

"Very unfortunate," concurred Sloan firmly, before the Superintendent could embark on a long recital of his running battles with the Watch Committee.

"In the circumstances," said Leeyes heavily.

"In the circumstances," agreed Sloan. Detective Inspector C. D. Sloan—Christopher Dennis to his wife and family—was inevitably known as "Seedy" to his friends. He was head of the tiny Criminal Investigation Department of the Berebury Division of the Calleshire Police Force and thus responsible to Superintendent Leeyes.

"And on top of everything else," said Leeyes in a tone pregnant with meaning.

"Quite so," said Detective Inspector Sloan.

"Just my luck," said Leeyes bitterly.

Detective Inspector Sloan refrained from pointing out that Detective Inspector Porritt of Calleford Division had been even more unlucky. What had happened to Trevor Porritt had been very unfortunate indeed. His investigation into the murder of Kenneth Carline completed and his full report on the case against Lucy Mirabel Durmast duly submitted, Detective Inspector Porritt had then, as was customary, returned to other duties.

It was in the executing of one of these that he had met with disaster. During the course of giving chase to one of Her Majesty's less lawful lieges Trevor Porritt had lost his footing and this had led to his undoing. He had promptly been hit on the head while he was down by the liege's partner in crime. Even more unfortunately he had been hit with the blunt instrument that had been intended for use on a night watchman at a superstore.

Since this assault upon his person Detective Inspector Trevor Porritt had not been the man he had been before and, alas, manifestly never would be again. The neurologists had said so. With unaccustomed unanimity, too. There had been no question of doctors differing and thus letting in a glimmer of hope. Henceforth, all the doctors said, Inspector Porritt would have a very short memory. What they did not tell his wife was quite how short that memory would be.

Like a minute.

Or that the hand that held the fork might forget the way to the mouth.

A cynic would have said that the real clue to the gravity of Inspector Porritt's condition lay in the studied kindness and courtesy which the medical profession extended to Mrs. Porritt. There were other pointers too. Especially in what was said about the future and, more important, what was left unsaid. There had been much talk of disability pensions and early retirement on health grounds and no mention at all of possible improvement and getting back to work in time.

"When shall we come back, Doctor?" a bemused Mrs. Porritt

had asked the hospital consultant. Trevor Porritt hadn't asked him anything at all.

Neurology is a speciality more concerned with diagnosis than with treatment—since so much neurological disorder is untreatable—but Mrs. Porritt was not to know that.

Yet.

It did mean, though, that the neurologist had his answer to her question off pat. "Your general practitioner will let me know if he wants me to see your husband again," he said with practised smoothness, ignoring an unresponsive Trevor altogether.

Mrs. Porritt had pulled herself together by then. "Like that, is it?" she said.

The neurologist had nodded slowly.

Inspector Porritt's wife had allowed her one and only touch of bitterness to creep in. "I get it, Doctor. You don't have to tell me. 'Don't call us, we'll call you.' That it?"

"I'm very much afraid so," said the other regretfully. Reality was meant to appear after the consultation when the expert would be at a safe distance from awkward questions—not during it when Olympian detachment might be threatened by the intrusion of real-life relatives with real-life questions to be answered.

Mrs. Porritt had taken Trevor home and set about the business of coming to terms with a different way of life from henceforth. Trevor himself had retreated into a private world inside his damaged brain and nobody knew what he thought any more. This was a pity, because by the time Lucy Mirabel Durmast had appeared in Court there were a number of questions Detective Inspector Sloan would have liked to have asked him.

It had been upon Detective Inspector Sloan that the case had devolved after Trevor Porritt had been injured. Sloan had dutifully read all the evidence that had been carefully assembled by his colleague. He had checked that it seemed all present and correct, forwarded it to the office of the Director of Public Prosecutions, and then forgotten all about it while he dealt with an outbreak of small but disturbingly skilful burglaries in Berebury's main shopping arcade.

And now the case had come to Court.

"Silence is consent," said the superintendent. His knowledge of law had a magpie quality about it and he had picked up the phrase from somewhere.

"Not in Court it isn't," responded Sloan with vigour. "She didn't even nod. That girl didn't consent to anything."

"What did she say when she was charged?" enquired the super-intendent with genuine professional interest. "People say funny things then," he added profoundly.

"They do," concurred Sloan. This was within his experience too. Someone should—probably would—write a book about them one day. The Charge Book at Berebury Police Station was full of the strange responses of those told that they were going to be pros-ecuted for misdemeanours of all kinds. To the real police cogno-scenti they were a true touchstone of guilt or innocence: in their way as revealing as litmus paper. The prompt and indignant "I never" was only sometimes genuine. The "Turned over two pages, have you, maybe?" seldom was. Sloan himself had only met the "You've got your duty to do, Officer" between the pages of prewar fiction but "It's a fair cop" did crop up from time to time.

So did "It's an unfair cop" or words to that effect. Usually ac-companied by threats to report the cop concerned to such national organisations as concerned themselves with attacking the police—and to the press, too, for good measure.

"Catch 'em by surprise," said the superintendent wistfully, "and you can sometimes be lucky." He was a great man himself for the immediate rather than the studied response.

"Only sometimes," said Sloan more cautiously. An officer had to be careful, though, about what could and what could not be con-strued as an admission of guilt. Being advised, with varying de-grees of explicitness, to tell it to the Marines, was one thing: listen-ing to a sobbing hulk of a man asking again and again "Why did she have to scream? I wouldn't have hit her if she hadn't screamed. She wouldn't stop . . ." was quite another.

"Telling them they weren't up to that sort of job sometimes does the trick," said the superintendent out of his own experience on the beat. "Gets them on the raw . . ."

The reverse of that particular coin, as Sloan knew only too well, was "Me, do a little job like that? I've got class, I have."

"Lucy Durmast didn't say anything when she was charged," said Detective Inspector Sloan. "That is to say," he added with pains-taking accuracy, "nothing that Trevor Porritt could catch. He made a note that she started to speak and then stopped in mid-breath."

"Not a lot of help," said Leeyes heavily.

"No." As far as Sloan was concerned nothing had been a lot of help in the case so far.

"And she hasn't said anything since?"

"Not a word."

"Not even to her solicitor?"

"She won't have one," replied Sloan succinctly.

"You can't altogether blame her for that, now can you, Sloan?" said Leeyes with unaccustomed jocularity.

"I understand, sir, quite informally, of course . . ."

"Of course . . ."

"That at the urgent request of Ronald Bolsover he's the deputy chairman of her father's firm—the senior partner of the family's solicitors—er—made himself available for consultation after she had been charged."

"She wouldn't talk to him?"

"She wouldn't even see him. Quite miffed about it, I'm told he was. She even sent him a message saying he wasn't to take any action whatsoever in any circumstances."

"She needn't have worried too much about that," said the superintendent. "Solicitors don't ever take action. All they do is suggest that you take it."

"There must have been something she didn't want him to do," said Sloan logically, "or she wouldn't have said so." It had been the only positive statement of any sort to be issued by Lucy Durmast and as such had been wrung dry of implications.

Leeyes grunted. "Bail? Did she ask for bail?"

"She didn't speak," Sloan reminded him.

"How did that affect bail?" asked Leeyes.

"Henry Simmonds had to ask his Clerk that," said Sloan.

"Ha! And what did he say?" pounced Leeyes. "He's supposed to know all the answers, isn't he?"

"The Clerk said that as no application had been made there was no way in which bail could be granted."

"Typical of the way the legal mind works," said Leeyes. "What about the police?"

"Had it been asked for," said Sloan slowly, "we would have opposed it . . ."

"Ah . . ."

"She was living alone, for one thing."

"Alone because she'd killed the chap she was living with?" suggested Leeyes. He, too, knew all about male murderers being mostly widowers.

"No, no," said Sloan hastily. "Nothing like that. She lives with her father . . . her mother's dead."

"But you said . . ."

"Her father's overseas at the moment. He's designing a new town in Africa."

"Haven't they got enough problems there already?"

"A town, not a township," responded Sloan absently. "She was living alone," he added, coming back to Lucy Durmast, "in a detached house in the village of Braffle Episcopi."

"That isn't exactly central either," grunted the superintendent. "Is it?"

"About as remote as you can get in East Calleshire," agreed Sloan feelingly. "Nearer to Calleford, of course, than to Berebury. The victim was taken to Calleford Hospital."

"Which is how Trevor Porritt came into the case, I suppose."

"His patch," agreed Detective Inspector Sloan, "not mine." He coughed. "The distance hasn't helped."

"Never does," said Leeyes bracingly. The superintendent himself seldom stepped out of his office at Berebury Police Station but was all in favour of everyone else's doing so.

"It isn't usual," Sloan said, "to bail people on murder charges anyway." A certain tenacity of purpose was needed sometimes to keep the superintendent to the point; equally he could on occasion be like a terrier who wouldn't let go. "Not," went on Sloan, "that I think she would have skipped it. Not the sort."

For someone who had remained totally silent throughout all manner of proceedings—legal and otherwise—Lucy Durmast had managed to project a very definite image.

Leeyes grunted again. "Let's get this quite straight, Sloan. The accused is alleged to have killed a man."

"Kenneth Malcolm Carline," supplied Sloan. That part was easy. There had been no difficulty at all in identifying the victim.

"And there was no doubt about how he died?"

"Not according to the Calleford pathologist." Sloan paused and added cautiously, "He's new and young, of course."

"That's a sight better than being old and hidebound," responded Leeyes crisply. "Naming no names, of course."

"Of course," agreed Sloan diplomatically. Dr. Dabbe, the Consultant Pathologist to the Berebury District Hospital Management Group, was neither young nor new at his job.

"What killed Carline?"

"Poison."

"A woman's way," mused Leeyes. It was a response that would have upset a great many campaigners for Women's Liberation.

"Yes, sir." Even the most committed defence lawyer would have had to agree that there were precedents for poison's being a woman's weapon.

"Who was he, then?" asked Leeyes. "The victim, I mean."

"A young man who worked for her father's firm."

"One of the old stories?" enquired Leeyes.

"Sir?"

"Him wanting to marry the boss's daughter and Daddy telling her she must and her not being keen."

"No, sir, it wasn't like that at all." There was a certain simplicity about famous legends that didn't equate with life.

"Sloan," said Leeyes unexpectedly, "you know there's a time in every fairy story when the frog turns into a prince?"

"Ye--es," agreed Sloan warily. The superintendent's discursiveness could lead anywhere. Anywhere at all.

"They've just discovered that there are some of those funny inheritance things—DNA molecules—in the phosphate in the skin of the frog."

"Really, sir?" said Sloan politely.

"Funny, that."

"Yes, sir."

"Especially when you think how often it was the frog that got turned into a prince."

"Yes, sir." He cleared his throat. "It wasn't like that at all with this young man Carline."

"No?"

"If you ask me," ventured Sloan consideringly, "it was more of a case of him not wanting to marry the boss's daughter."

"Doesn't happen so often, of course," commented Leeyes sagely. "It's the quickest ladder to the top."

"What I mean is," amplified Sloan, "that Kenneth Carline had just announced his engagement to someone else."

"And instead of saying 'Hard Cheddar' to herself, this Durmast girl reaches for the arsenic?"

"Not exactly, sir," temporised Sloan. By any standard that was an over-simplification.

"Well, I'm not to know, Sloan, am I, unless you tell me?" said Leeyes. "Calleford Division handed the whole case over as a package after Trevor Porritt got hurt." He sniffed ominously. "It was meant to be a complete package, too, with no loose ends. That's what they said."

"Trevor Porritt didn't leave any loose ends," insisted Sloan. "Calleford said it was all cut and dried and it looked as if it was."

"What's the difficulty then?" demanded Leeyes.

"There isn't one as far as I know," said Sloan, hanging on to the shreds of his patience with an effort.

"Except that she won't talk."

"That's not our problem," said Sloan. "That's someone else's."

The someone else whose problem in due course the silence of Lucy Durmast became was Judge Eddington.

His Honour sat in the Crown Court in the county town of Calleford. The scenario there had some of the same components as those of the Magistrates' Court at Berebury but there were some important differences too. There was a certain amount of ceremonial rising and bowing for one thing. The judge was robed and the barristers were gowned for another.

The prisoner was dressed exactly as she had been before.

The judges and counsel were wigged.

The prisoner's hair gleamed like burnished copper.

The skin of the judge was like old, creased parchment. The prisoner had the sort of skin that looked—given sunshine—as if it would freckle easily. There was no sunshine in prison. Confinement there had done nothing to bring freckles out and her complexion looked instead only rather pale under that striking hair.

The judge listened to the formalities with which the trial began with the impassivity of long practice, settling himself into a state of mind in which he could listen to all the evidence with total impartiality. He watched in silence while the Clerk of the Court endeavoured to get Lucy Durmast to plead. Judge Eddington had met mutism before.

He gave no sign of this—nor of whether or not he had taken note

of the fact that the Attorney General had apparently waived his
traditional right of prosecution in cases of alleged murder by
poisoning. He let the Clerk work his way through the proper pro-
cedures without interference and when this, too, resulted only in
total silence on the part of the prisoner the judge then—and only
then—drew breath to speak.

He proceeded to do what many another professional man would
also have dearly liked to have been able to do when confronted
with a difficult woman. And in so doing he followed a well-worn
track.

"Remanded for psychiatric report," he said briskly. "Next case,
please."

THREE

Haustus—Draughts

Lucy Durmast kept on telling herself to try to think of the encounter as a game. If only she could do that she would be able to keep her mind clear. And she certainly needed to keep her mind clear if she were going to outwit the psychiatrist seated opposite her. She clasped her hands tightly together in her lap and fixed her eyes unwaveringly on his face.

The psychiatrist automatically registered the clenched hands and much else besides. He purposely hadn't allowed the need for speech to arise as Lucy Durmast had been brought into the consulting room, busying himself instead with the formalities of divesting her of her coat, getting her seated and reading through her file.

"Let me see now," he began in the manner of an ordinary doctor at an ordinary consultation, "you've been having some trouble lately, haven't you?"

Even in a prison setting, noted Lucy Durmast drily to herself, the habit of meiosis didn't desert the medical profession. Her grandfather had been a doctor and he, too, had always preferred understatement. A patient's being "not too well," had, in his canon, meant a death knell.

"Trouble does sometimes affect the capacity for speech," the man opposite continued easily. "To put it very simply the brain pulls down a shutter on the past to protect itself from unpleasant memories."

She stared at him, trying not to scream that it hadn't done any such thing: that she remembered with searing clarity everything that had happened the day that Kenneth Carline had died.

"Especially," the psychiatrist went on, "when the past has got something in it that you particularly don't want to remember."

Had Lucy Durmast permitted herself the luxury of speech this would have been the point at which she would have positively exploded that chance. She wasn't going to—and anyway never would be able to—forget the sickening sequence of events of that day last January.

"You can't always choose," he explained, "what you want to remember and what you want to forget."

She blinked. There was a poem, wasn't there, about that. Where you could remember if you wanted to. Or forget. Lucy Durmast fixed her gaze on the wall behind the psychiatrist's head and concentrated her mind on Christina Rossetti's Song: "When I am Dead."

> And if thou wilt, remember,
> And if thou wilt, forget.

For all the sentiment in her verse Lucy Durmast suspected that Christina Rossetti had been a tougher personality than the casual reader might have thought.

"If you could just cough for me," the psychiatrist was saying almost apologetically, "it would save us from having to examine your mouth and throat and so forth."

One of the many things Lucy Durmast had learnt at her grandfather's knee had been that the first duty of every psychiatrist had been to exclude real physical illness: organic disease that wasn't the opposite of inorganic but of mental or psychosomatic disorder. This school of thought was reflected rather neatly in Army Regulations. A soldier who reported sick was deemed to be on a charge until he had been demonstrated to have a physical illness. She coughed without shifting her gaze from him and continued to think about Christina Rossetti. There had been more lines in the poem about choosing. She concentrated on the poem with a frown.

> Haply I may remember
> And haply may forget.

Those alternatives certainly did not apply in this case. She could neither haply forget nor haply remember the last time she had seen Kenneth Carline.

No, that wasn't true.

To be absolutely precise there had been nothing actually memorable about his last visit. It had been what had come after that last visit that had been so shattering. So shattering that she had come to think of it in her mind as Black Monday: the day that Kenneth Carline had come to the Old Rectory at Braffle Episcopi for a quick luncheon . . .

The psychiatrist had only registered the frown. In spite of all his training and expertise, thought Lucy Durmast, he wasn't really a mind reader. "Coughing didn't hurt, did it?" he asked quickly.

He very nearly caught her off guard then. She had begun to shake her head almost automatically before she remembered that a state of non-communication was supposed to exist between Lucy Durmast and the rest of the world.

"That's good," said the psychiatrist matter-of-factly. "If you had had any pain or couldn't cough we might be thinking of a clinical condition."

What had provoked Lucy Durmast's frown had been her recollection of the meal that she had given Kenneth Carline on that Black Monday. Even "meal" was really too grand a word for the few ingredients that she had put together at short notice after he had telephoned her to say he was coming over to Braffle Episcopi to collect some of her father's architectural drawings to do with the Palshaw to Edsway Tunnel from his study at the Old Rectory. It was very difficult to believe that there had been something in that meal that had killed him. But everyone insisted that there had. It hadn't helped, of course, that she had so meticulously cleared everything away afterwards.

At the time, naturally, she had known of no reason why she shouldn't . . .

"If you haven't got anything in the way of physical reasons to account for your—er—speechlessness," said the psychiatrist, choosing his words with care, "there is a possibility that you are experiencing what we call conversion symptoms . . ."

Why, she wondered, didn't he call her silence hysterical aphonia and have done with it? Her grandfather had never trifled with lay expressions when he talked to her. Dr. Durmast had always used the grand Latin names for the diseases that described the thousand shocks the flesh is heir to—usually in words borrowed from the Greeks who had spotted them first.

"These conversion symptoms can make speech difficult," the doctor opposite her now explained, searching in his own mind for some suitable *point d'appui* at which to begin. "To put it very simply . . ."

Lucy Durmast listened with detachment while he set out in words something she already knew.

"Occasionally," he pontificated, "the mind converts some shock or other that it has received into a physical symptom rather than a mental one.

Some shock, thought Lucy, summed up very nicely her sudden arrest on a charge of murdering Kenneth Carline—poor hardworking Kenneth Carline, his feet barely on the bottom rung of the civil-engineering ladder but very keen to climb it.

Some chicken, some neck, in fact.

The psychiatrist had steepled his fingers. "Especially when the patient is trying to solve a conflict by repression," he said.

At least, she thought, he called her a patient rather than a prisoner. That was something she had begun to value.

"And the physical symptom only goes away when the repression has been dealt with and the conflict settled," said the psychiatrist. "I am sure as an intelligent young woman you can understand all this."

She managed not to nod. She gave him all her attention though. And tried hard to remember all the tales her grandfather had told her. Like Sir Walter Scott's grandfather, her own grandfather had been great on tales. During the last war old Dr. Durmast had conducted hundreds of medical examinations of conscripts called up for military duty and she had been reared on the tricks practised by both sides.

Not all the conscripts had been equally anxious to serve King and Country. Some feigned blindness and others deafness. The pseudo-blind were usually easily caught out by the simple device of letting the doctor's pen roll towards the edge of the desk in their direction. Few had enough time in which to steel themselves to resist the impulse to put out a hand to catch it. The voluntarily deaf could be unexpectedly startled without difficulty. She couldn't now remember the methods resorted to that had lured unwilling soldiers into betraying that they could speak . . .

Which was a pity.

The psychiatrist continued in the same vein about her not wanting to remember the past. "We are only talking about a symptom, of course," he said fairly, "and not the cause of that symptom.

Only when that cause has been dealt with could you be considered cured."

She fixed him with her eye at that.

"As long as anxiety and fear persist which derive from completely repressed or dissociated memories which cannot be faced," he pronounced, "then the risk of the symptoms returning will exist."

At least, decided Lucy, he was being honest with her.

"I don't think I can tell you any more than this." He gave her a tiny smile. "Only that the mind is a very, very complicated organ but"—he blinked—"I'm sure that you know that already."

The psychiatrist was projecting every indication he could of a man honestly trying to be helpful, but Lucy Durmast still did not relax.

"Is there anything you would like to ask me?" he continued, pushing a note pad and pen in her direction. "You could write it down if you would rather do that."

She made no move at all.

"Or perhaps draw how you feel?" he suggested. "Some people find that easier. No? Very well, then." He rose to his feet. "If you should change your mind and want to see me at any time I will arrange to be told."

In the end he caught her out with one of the oldest tricks in the trade.

He took her coat off the hook by the door and courteously held it out behind her for her to slip on.

"Thank you," said Lucy Durmast aloud quite without thinking.

A good sauce might well be described as gravy raised to a higher power: the same could almost be said about judges and magistrates.

Judge Eddington sat in Calleford Crown Court without the need to consult the Clerk on points of law, and without having to secure the agreement of his fellow members of the Bench to his judgements. The jury made up its own mind with such assistance as he deemed it appropriate for him to give it. There was no retiring to go into conclave about the fine detail, so to speak, with the other magistrates: only an appeal to a higher court where both his judgements and sentence awarded could be overturned.

The process was called certiorari and it served to keep a man on his mettle.

The judge remembered Lucy Mirabel Durmast's first appearance before him. Now she was back again, this time with reports of one kind and another. Judge Eddington read them with care. There was one from the psychiatrist written upon his soul and conscience—an interesting batting order, that—stating that in his professional view the accused was not deaf and was not suffering from nervous aphonia, hysterical mutism or congenital dumbness. There was another report from the Prison Governor confirming that in her own best interests Lucy Durmast had again been offered the services of a duty solicitor but had remained mute.

The Clerk went into his set piece again.

As before Lucy Durmast kept her silence.

Judge Eddington crackled the reports before him as he spoke to the prisoner. "You have been found sane and fit to plead," he said in tones of measured solemnity. "If there is any reason why you do not wish to do so I would be willing to know what it is."

In the words of the time-honoured music-hall joke, no answer was the stern reply.

"I am advised," continued Judge Eddington, "that you are neither deaf nor dumb. If you insist that this is the case I must ask you to make some sign to this effect."

Detective Inspector Sloan, who was also in Court, hoped that the judge wasn't tempting Providence. A gamut of riotous possibilities ran through his mind—from Hitler salutes through Masonic signs to the more arcane signals of the Scout Movement.

Lucy Durmast remained both silent and still.

The judge collected his thoughts and, as was his wont, marshalled his words with care before he spoke. He took his time about it: celerity had no part in the due processes of the Law. Haste, in his mind, was synonymous with lynch law and there would be none of that in any court in which he, Cedric Eddington, sat. He was as impervious to the pressure of time as to any other pressure that Defence or Prosecution or Press cared to try to apply to him. His freedom from attack upon his person in taking this view stretched a long way back into England's history. His freedom from anxiety in dispensing justice belonged to a more personal cast of mind. And if his day's work meant that some of those standing in the dock before him went that night to prison, then so be it. He would lose no sleep about it. That, after all, was what he was there for.

He cleared his throat. "I must therefore reluctantly conclude that you are being mute of malice."

Lucy Durmast very nearly shouted from the dock that she wasn't. Malice didn't come into it. At least, she corrected herself in her own mind, not on her part. Malice there must have been on somebody's part, because Kenneth Carline had been poisoned. The police pathologist had said so. Hyoscine hydrobromide had been found in Kenneth's body in a quantity sufficient to kill. Presumably somebody somewhere had raised the possibility of its being there by accident—and discounted that alternative. Otherwise she, Lucy Durmast, wouldn't be standing where she was today.

"And furthermore"—Judge Eddington was still talking—"I must warn you that you are in grave danger of being in contempt of court."

How like a man, thought Lucy, to put an institution like the Court upon such a pedestal. If you didn't agree to play by their rules, then they took their bat home. In the case of poor Kenneth Carline it would have been a ball rather than a bat, of course. Rugby had been his game. He had been very keen on Rugby. In fact he had been so mauled and bruised when he had turned up at Braffle Episcopi that Black Monday by the previous Saturday afternoon's game that she would have been less surprised to learn that it was that that had killed him rather than poison.

But it had been poison.

The police had said so.

And kept on saying so.

"And if I do find you in contempt of court," Judge Eddington's voice broke into her reverie, "then I must advise you that I have the power to commit you to prison until such time as you have purged your contempt."

Whether it worried him at all to send a person to prison was the question the Judge was asked most often in the outside world. (It was a sad but true reflection on that same world that few dinner partners enquired if he ever worried about sentencing the innocent.) He always replied that it never troubled him to send the guilty to prison—but the point was usually lost upon them. Judge Eddington never explained why it was that he didn't mind and he was seldom asked. By then anyway his fellow guests had usually got past the soup course and onto the weather or the Government . . .

In the dim and distant past when Cedric Eddington had been up at Cambridge he had read neither Classics nor Law but Archeology and Anthropology. It had proved a surprisingly good grounding for the judiciary: the proper study of mankind being man. Or in his case, Man. A working knowledge of the territorial imperative, for instance, went a long way towards making the Laws relating to the Ownership of Property intelligible . . . And when he had come down from Cambridge—at a time when his fellow undergraduates were hiking across the Sahara or back-packing in the Carpathian Mountains—he had gone, on his father's advice, to Italy.

"Surely Roman Law can wait," the young Cedric Eddington had protested when the Italian visit had first been bruited.

Eddington *père*, it transpired, had not had Roman Law in mind as education. It had been Florence he had been thinking of, not Rome, and to Florence a jejune but open-minded Cedric Eddington had duly gone. He had come back with a greater understanding of the ways of the world. In Florence he had seen pictures of just and unjust Judges, of Vice and Virtue, of Heaven and Hell, of Calumny and the Naked Truth, of Paradise and Purgatory. Good and evil had been polarised in Cedric Eddington's mind forever.

And so had something else.

However long he spent in the Courts of Law he would never make the mistake of asking a woman how she had come to the life of the oldest profession. He had heard that answer too. "Luck, my lord. Pure luck."

"I repeat," he said now to Lucy Durmast, "that I have the power to commit you to prison for contempt of court and I shall not hesitate to do so if I find that you have no sound reason for not speaking."

He hadn't meant to say "no sound reason," thought Lucy. This was no time for legal puns though and not even the flicker of a smile crossed her face.

The best reason that Judge Eddington knew for sending a man to prison was seldom even acknowledged by the reformers. In his view it was to save other members of the tribe from having to have converse with the sinner. It was, in fact, the tribe that was being spared, not the sinner being punished. To his way of thinking, the avoidance of the newly bereaved came into the same category. It, too, was primitive, indeed instinctive, behaviour. So, too, was the shunning of the halt and the lame and the dying. That was what animals did. The feeble immediately became outcasts of the pack for reasons directly related to the survival of the pack.

Judge Eddington saw his sentencing of those who had offended against tribal customs or Society's code—call such ways by any name—as a late form of banishment. He was with William Shakespeare in this. The most condign punishment that the Bard had envisaged for his historical character had been the order to eschew the realm and become an outcast from the people of their own land. Sending someone to Coventry was the same thing in minuscule. There had been old laws, too, even earlier than those in Shakespeare's day, about those newly sentenced to exile sticking to the King's Highway until the coast was reached that still sent a shudder through the imagination.

"I am informed," continued Cedric Eddington dispassionately, "that you are perfectly capable of hearing what I am saying . . ."

Lucy did not move.

He fixed her with a beady eye. "And I am warning you for the last time that if you continue to keep silence I shall have no hesitation in returning you to prison."

Into Lucy Durmast's mind floated the memory of a book she had once read with the peerless title of *A Time to Keep Silence*. There was a time and a place for everything, of course. What the judge was saying so weightily was that silence when one had been charged in a Court of Law was more than a little inappropriate. A sort of not playing the game to their rules or something, thought Lucy vaguely. Men were such funny creatures.

"Is that quite clear?" he thundered towards the dock.

She said nothing.

"Lucy Durmast," said Judge Eddington, lending each and every syllable as much weight as he could, "I must warn you that if you persist in being mute of malice that you stand not only in danger of going back to prison for contempt of court . . ."

She looked up but said nothing.

". . . but also," continued the judge severely, "of not receiving that justice to which you are entitled."

She wanted to cry out that there had been no justice in her arrest but she didn't.

"And," finished Judge Eddington impressively, "which it is my duty to see that you are afforded."

Lucy Durmast's immediate thought was that he was going to
have his work cut out to do that—but she kept her lips firmly
together and did not voice it.

"Sentenced to seven days imprisonment for contempt of court,"
pronounced Judge Eddington.

"Playing for time, I suppose," sniffed Superintendent Leeyes, to
whom this news was relayed by Detective Inspector Sloan.

"Who is?" asked Inspector Harpe of Traffic Division who had
come back to the police station from the Court with Detective
Inspector Sloan.

"The pair of them," snarled Leeyes.

"The pair?" began Sloan. "But, sir . . ."

"The judge for one," said the Superintendent. "You can bet your
sweet life he's been trying to find out behind the scenes what it's
all about. He's not silly."

"He has been keeping in touch with the prison," admitted Sloan
slowly.

"There! What did I tell you?" Leeyes glared at his two subordi-
nates. "I said he was playing for time."

"They've told him," said Sloan, "that she's played possum all the
while there too."

"Dumb crambo, more like," said Leeyes.

"Some sort of funny game," agreed Sloan, who wasn't too sure
that he could remember the details of dumb crambo.

"And the girl as well," insisted Leeyes. "In my opinion she's
playing for time too."

"Quite possibly, sir," agreed Sloan.

"Though you can search me why she bothers."

"Perhaps, sir, it isn't actually time she's playing for," suggested
Sloan.

"What other sort of stakes do you have in mind?" enquired
Leeyes frostily.

"All the while you're actually in prison," replied Sloan, "you are
quite safe physically yourself."

"Except from other prisoners," put in Inspector Harpe with an
accuracy based on realism. Inspector Harpe was in charge of Traffic Division at Berebury. He was universally known throughout
the Calleshire Force as Happy Harry because he had never been

known to smile. He on his part maintained that there had never been anything about which to be cheerful in Traffic Division.

"Other prisoners, Harry," pointed out Sloan, "may sometimes be less of a risk than something or someone in the outside world."

"Who and what?" demanded Leeyes upon the instant. "Tell me that, Sloan."

"I don't know, sir." Sloan turned back to the Superintendent. "Trevor Porritt must have thought he had a water-tight case or he wouldn't have proceeded with it."

"They do say he was a cautious man," conceded Leeyes.

"But," said Sloan, "I, of course, only know what he wrote down. He can't remember anything now."

Leeyes grunted.

"I suppose the accused can choose to keep quiet if they want to," remarked Inspector Harpe with all the relaxation of one who is not directly involved with a case. "After all, it's a free country, isn't it?"

Since this last was one of Superintendent Leeyes's perennial hobby-horses, Sloan sought a swift diversion. "What were you doing in Court today, Harry?"

The Traffic Inspector lifted his head like a melancholy St. Bernard seeking a reassuring pat. "Couple of cowboy drivers got their lorries tangled up in the Palshaw Tunnel. Both exceeding the speed limit at the time, so it served 'em right."

"Anything to say for themselves?" barked Leeyes. He disapproved of articulated vehicles on principle.

"Not a lot," said Happy Harry. "One was French . . ."

"Ah . . ." breathed Leeyes vengefully. Heavy goods vehicles did little for the Entente Cordiale at any time: and after a Road Traffic Accident nothing at all.

". . . and the other German," finished Harpe.

Leeyes lost interest.

Sloan said, "Harry, you saw this girl Lucy Durmast, didn't you? What did you make of her?"

The verdict of Inspector Harold Harpe of Traffic Division came without hesitation or equivocation. "Nice legs," he said.

FOUR

Auristillae—Ear-drops

Superintendent Leeyes glanced ominously at his watch. "If we've got to do Calleford's dirty work for them I suppose we'd better do it properly. You'll have to make do with Crosby, though. I can't spare anyone better. I take it, Sloan, that you've already been over Inspector Porritt's report in detail?"

Detective Inspector Sloan wondered for a moment if Lucy Durmast's silence had cost her as much effort in Court as his own restraint quite often did with Superintendent Leeyes. He contented himself now with saying after a pause, "I have, sir."

"Let me get it quite straight, then," said Leeyes, adding acidly, "now that Inspector Harpe has seen fit to go back to his proper duties."

"There isn't a lot of problem about the evidence, sir," said Sloan.

"Except," supplied Leeyes, "that for some reason nobody can get round to presenting it."

"Quite so, sir."

"Well?"

"It's really quite simple, sir . . ."

Leeyes snorted.

Sloan reached for Trevor Porritt's file. "Kenneth Carline had lunch with Lucy Durmast on Monday, January 13, and died later that evening from poisoning by hyoscine hydrobromide."

"If that's your nutshell, Sloan," said Leeyes unkindly, "there isn't enough in it."

"Carline didn't eat anything before he got to her father's house and he didn't eat anything after leaving it and before he died."

Leeyes grunted. "That's been proved, has it, Sloan?"

"He had his breakfast as usual with the three other young men with whom he shared a flat . . ."

"And they were all all right?"

"Fit as fleas." Sloan coughed. "They—these four—had a rota for the—er—domestic side."

"That makes a change," said Leeyes. "They usually have a girl-friend."

Sloan forged on. "It wasn't Kenneth Carline's turn to do the cooking anyway that week. He ate what all the others ate and left for work as usual."

"Where's work as usual?"

"Messrs. William Durmast, Civil Engineers, in Calleford. Their offices are in that big old house in the Rushmarket. Quite a nice place, really. Central and so forth."

"Being central," said Leeyes realistically, "usually means that there's nowhere to park."

Sloan continued his narrative. "All that Kenneth Carline had there was coffee from a common source within the office shared by everyone. One of those help-yourself machines. To make things simpler still, he had it black and almost as soon as he got to the office."

"Most young men need pulling together on Monday mornings."

"He had had a bit of a trouncing anyway in a Rugby match on the Saturday afternoon," contributed Sloan, consulting the file. "Trevor Porritt had established that because at the post-mortem the pathologist found a lot of . . . of . . . eccymoses."

"If doctors mean bruises," grumbled Leeyes, "I don't know why they don't say so. Got to prove they've had an expensive education or something."

"The bruises were all at least forty-eight hours old though," said Sloan, "and so didn't come into the picture."

Leeyes grunted. "Go on."

"After he'd had his coffee Carline went into the office of the deputy chairman. That's a man called Ronald Bolsover."

"The man who tried to persuade Lucy Durmast to see a solicitor?"

"That's right, sir," Sloan nodded. "He's in charge of the firm while William Durmast—he's the girl's father—is in Africa and Carline had an appointment with him for eleven o'clock that morning in his office."

"Then he could have . . ."

"Ronald Bolsover's office is one of those old-fashioned ones where the walls are glass above waist level," said Sloan.

"None of this open-plan nonsense, then," grunted Leeyes, "with potted palms pretending to be walls."

A memory from *A Midsummer Night's Dream* to do with Snout serving the office of a wall welled up in Sloan's mind, but he instantly suppressed it. There was a time and a place for everything. "No, sir," he said. "Nothing like that. I understand it's something to do with needing all the light the rooms can get for technical drawings."

"Artists need plenty of north light, too," Leeyes informed him gratuitously. The superintendent was a great one for attending adult-education evening classes, and one winter there had been one on the life and art of Rubens. The lecturer had done his best but had not been able to prevent Superintendent Leeyes from taking a purely police view of the great Peter Paul.

"Anyway," said Sloan, valiantly sticking to the point, "the deputy chairman's secretary was in the next office all the time that Kenneth Carline was with Ronald Bolsover."

"And?"

"And although nobody could hear what they were saying, she is prepared to swear that neither Mr. Bolsover nor Kenneth Carline ate or drank anything while they were there together."

"There are plenty of places to stop between Calleford and Braffle Episcopi," said Leeyes. "It's right over on the coast, don't forget."

"I know, sir. Between Marby and Edsway."

"Well?"

"Time came into it, sir."

"Swallowing something doesn't take long."

"That would only be if it were suicide, sir," said Sloan, "and he hadn't gone into a pub or cafe." Superintendent Leeyes was given to picking holes in most arguments. The trouble was that he usually found them where no one else had thought to look.

"Time wouldn't have been of the essence then," pointed out Leeyes.

"No, sir, it wouldn't," Sloan agreed. Who had it been who had gone to the water's edge and decided that there was after all no hurry about drowning herself and had something to eat? A girl in a book Sloan had had to read for a school examination once a long time ago—could it have been Maggie Tulliver? He'd always meant one day to go back and read something else that the same author had written but somehow he just hadn't the time. Silly, really, when you thought about the years in between.

"But," barked Leeyes, breaking into his reverie, "time mattered, did it?"

"Carline was working to a pretty tight schedule that morning." Leeyes grunted.

"As it is, sir, he must have covered the ground between Calleford and Braffle Episcopi well over the speed limit anyway."

"Inspector Harpe's merry men had all gone to lunch, I suppose," said Leeyes, "seeing as it was between twelve and three."

"There certainly wasn't time for the deceased to have stopped at a pub or cafe that morning en route and still got where he did when he did," said Sloan. "Anyway, Inspector Porritt checked them all out and they swear Carline hadn't been in."

"How do you know when he got there?" demanded Leeyes. "I thought you said the girl was living in the house there alone. If there's only her word for it . . ."

"One of the men at the tunnel at Palshaw saw him go through just before one o'clock. Apparently Carline shouted to the chap that he would be back at two and carried on. The workman knew Carline quite well by sight, of course, from working on the tunnel."

Leeyes grunted. "Braffle Episcopi's near enough to the Edsway end of the tunnel."

"That's why the girl's father bought a house there in the first place."

"What is why?" asked Leeyes grumpily.

"William Durmast is the civil engineer who was awarded the contract to design and build the Palshaw to Edsway Tunnel . . ." Sloan hesitated. He wasn't at all sure if "build" was the right word for putting in a tunnel. A better one was probably "construct."

Or dig.

Or sink.

"And this Lucy is his daughter and she is supposed to have done for Kenneth Carline?"

"Yes, sir." Sloan hesitated. "At least, that's what Trevor Porritt thought."

"Beyond reasonable doubt?" enquired Leeyes, investing the phrase with all its legal significance.

"Inspector Porritt thought so," said Sloan, "or he wouldn't have proceeded."

Leeyes grunted. "I don't know what sort of standards they have in Calleford Division."

Detective Inspector Sloan of Berebury Division carefully laid the file on the death of Kenneth Carline back on the desk, and said, "Good enough for a warrant."

It was this very same point that Ronald Bolsover was making to his wife. They were going over the ground for the hundredth time.

"You can say what you like about Lucy," Bolsover said, "but she's not silly. She knows as well as anyone what would happen if her father found out about . . . about . . . well, all this."

"He'd come home," said Mrs. Bolsover.

"Exactly."

"At once."

"On the next plane," agreed her husband. "And what would happen at Mgongwala if he did?"

Phyllis Bolsover was renowned for her lack of interest in her husband's business affairs but even she could answer that question. "Nothing, I suppose."

"Precisely," said Ronald Bolsover. "Nothing at all. Not a single thing." The building contract for the new capital city of the emergent African state of Dlasa had specified the number of Dlasa tribesmen to be employed in its construction, and the Dlasa were not renowned for either their industry or their technical competence. The same contract had required the number of foreign technicians to be kept to a minimum. (There had been no mention at all of the number of Thecats to be given work, since they were an oppressed minority in Dlasa.) "The cement would be unworkable in a week for a start," added Bolsover, "and their ideas about preserving wood date back to the Ark. Actually Noah would have made a better all-round job anyway."

"Bill's got help out there," pointed out Phyllis Bolsover, who hadn't much of a sense of humour. "He's not the only one in Dlasa."

"Only Bill has managed to get through to the Chancellor fellow who really runs the show."

"But I thought that the King . . ."

"King Thabile III," said Ronald Bolsover bitterly, "listens to his Chancellor and to practically no one else." Politics came into building contracts as they did into everything else—especially building contracts for new capital cities.

"Surely," said his wife, "they would understand if Bill explained about his daughter needing him."

"Girls don't have the same standing in Dlasa as they do in our culture." He paused and revised this. "Actually, when it comes to the point, they don't feel the same way about children anyway as we do in the West." He had to choose his words with care. The Bolsovers had no family. Phyllis Bolsover did have a very fine collection of Bow china though; her husband's pride and joy was an elaborate greenhouse of exotic plants. "I'm sure I don't know why I'm saying the West. Dlasa's more south than east of here . . ."

"I don't see why . . ." she began to object.

"Moreover," he said, "nobody could possibly describe the Dlasa as even remotely monogamous . . ."

"On the contrary," she responded tartly, "if even half of what I've heard is true." To Phyllis Bolsover, the idea of six children was seven too many.

"So they've all got—er—quiverfuls of sons," said Ronald Bolsover, "which is what matters to them, and daughters only if they're unlucky."

"Unlucky?" Even Phyllis Bolsover lifted her head at that.

"Dowry comes expensive in Dlasa."

Her face cleared. "Dowry? These days? I didn't realise that they were as backward as that." She didn't remember what she had brought to their marriage and in any case hadn't seen it as such.

"So," he carried on, explaining, "a daughter in trouble wouldn't signify with the Dlasa."

"But trouble with the law is rather different," she protested.

"Actually," he said, "they don't have a lot of that out there."

"Of what?"

"Law," said Bolsover neatly. "King Thabile is an absolute monarch." The background reading for the Mgongwala contract had been very comprehensive. "That means his word is law." The full significance of the phrase struck Ronald Bolsover for the first time.

"What he says goes, then?" said his wife, summing up the Divine Right of Kings in a single phrase.

"Thabile Rules O.K.," assented Bolsover, relaxing suddenly. "Actually I understand from Bill that what Hamish Mgambo . . . that's the Chancellor . . ."

"Hamish?" She lifted a well-groomed eyebrow.

"They had missionaries."

"There, too?"

"Scots ones." He nodded and went on, "It's what this Mgambo fellow suggests to the King that is really what goes." Reality and political theory seldom went hand-in-hand without complications.

"And you think that that is why Lucy's spinning all this out?" asked Phyllis.

"Lord knows, she understands how important the building of Mgongwala is to the firm. After all, she's a substantial shareholder in her own right because of what her mother left." He frowned. "I know it's not a Canberra or a Brasília but as far as the fortunes of William Durmast of Calleford are concerned it's the setting seal." Ronald Bolsover had never done other than identify with the company: he was as proud of it as its owner. "The Mgongwala contract couldn't have come at a better time after finishing the Palshaw Tunnel either. You know that."

Phyllis Bolsover sniffed. "Well, I'm sure if I were Lucy just at this particular time I'd want someone around taking a proper interest."

"She wouldn't see old Puckle, the solicitor, she wouldn't see Cecelia Allsworthy, who's her best friend, and she wouldn't see me," he said again for the hundredth time. "And when she was asked if there was anyone else she did want to see she wouldn't answer. You can make what you like of that."

"She knows what she's doing," said Mrs. Bolsover consideringly. "I'm quite sure about that."

"Yes," agreed Bolsover. "And that's what I'm counting on, because one thing is quite certain and that is that one of the Durmasts—*père ou fille*—is going to hold me wrong. As I see it, I'm on a hiding to nothing for not cabling Bill and worse from Lucy if I do."

"You'd have thought the newspapers . . ."

Her husband snorted gently. "A runner with a cleft stick would have his work cut out to get to Mgongwala."

"Dlasa's got an airport—all right, all right—a landing strip, then."

"I daresay that the British envoy there gets the English Top Newspaper by air in due course but Lucy's case hasn't hit the headlines yet, has it? Besides . . ." he hesitated.

"Besides?"

"Our envoy wants Mgongwala finished as quickly as possible, too."

"Why?"

"There were a couple of Iron Curtain country tenders for building it. Bill only got the contract for Britain by the skin of his teeth."

Phyllis Bolsover came back to Lucy Durmast. "She's of age," she said, again not for the first time. "I suppose that means she can do as she wants."

"What you really mean, my dear," he said drily, "is that she's an Englishwoman born in wedlock with her feet on dry land and therefore has nothing to fear."

It was no accident that Bill Durmast was representing the firm in Dlasa. Ronald Bolsover would never have been able to establish a rapport with King Thabile's Chancellor as Bill Durmast had done, let alone with King Thabile. His wasn't that sort of a personality. He was the firm's technical expert.

"And this isn't Africa." His wife was incurably European. The epitome of English civilisation to Phyllis Bolsover was a fine piece of porcelain from Stratford-le-Bow.

"I know," he said wearily. This ground, too, had been gone over time and again by the pair of them. "This is twentieth-century England."

Phyllis Bolsover voiced the thought that had worried her most. "The police seem so very sure about everything."

Bolsover shrugged his shoulders. "They've got a long stop, which makes it easier for them."

"I know that the last analysis comes in Court," she said almost crossly, "but all the same . . ."

"And that's where Lucy won't have any help." His worry surfaced too.

Perversely Mrs. Bolsover said she could understand that. "Lawyers always make such a meal of the simplest little thing."

"Murder," he responded colourlessly, "may be simple but it's not little."

She made a gesture of impatience. "You know what I mean, Ronald."

Bolsover shifted the conversational ground slightly. "Why she had to give Kenneth Carline the sort of food she did beats me all the same," he said. "Asking for trouble."

"Oh, I don't know . . ."

"Hang it all, he only rang the girl at practically the last minute."

"So she didn't have a lot of time," said his wife.

"Time or not, I don't call chili con carne a scratch meal."

"It is," she said absently.

"Unfortunately," he went on as if she hadn't spoken, "nobody can deny it has a flavour to cover a multitude of sins."

"I don't suppose at the best of times the meat comes particularly fresh down Mexico way," said Phyllis Bolsover. "The worst of times doesn't bear thinking about." She shuddered. "The great thing about France is that they understand about food." The Bolsovers had a holiday home in Provence.

"And why serve him that damn silly vegetable into the bargain?" he demanded. "You know, the one that sounds like a piece of jewellery."

"Samphire."

"I ask you! Samphire on a Monday morning in winter."

"Lucy told you herself before she turned into a clam," his wife reminded him patiently, "that she'd been experimenting with freezing it and thought she knew Kenneth well enough to try it out on him."

"Poor man's asparagus," he said scornfully. "What's that to give a man?"

"I believe it's quite nice," said his wife calmly. "It would go well with a powerful flavour like chili con carne. So would the beer she gave him."

"And so would hyoscine," said Ronald Bolsover soberly. "At least, that's what the police say."

FIVE

Applicationes—Applications

As it happened the police were saying something even more to the point.

At least, one member of the force was.

"What, sir?" echoed Detective Constable Crosby to Detective Inspector Sloan, to whose room he had been summoned. "Check out a murder case against the clock?"

"Lucy Durmast's got seven days," said Sloan succinctly, "and so have we."

"Somebody else's case, too."

"Could happen to anyone."

"And in somebody else's division," said the constable, in whom the territorial imperative was as strong as in any man.

"Calleford," said Sloan briskly, "is less than half the County away." Constable Crosby was very nearly as insular in outlook as the superintendent.

"Mission impossible," declared the detective constable to Sloan.

"It better hadn't be," responded that worthy vigorously. "Or Superintendent Leeyes will want to know the reason why."

"The trail's cold, for one thing," complained the constable. "All this happened last January."

"Time and crime," said Sloan neatly, "can't always be separated."

"But it's not like detecting something that has just happened," insisted Crosby, aggrieved.

"More of a challenge, that's all."

"And the accused's not giving us any help, is she?"

"She doesn't have to," said Sloan. "It is a cardinal principle of English law that the accused doesn't have to defend him or herself against a charge."

"All the same . . ."

"The burden of proof rests entirely on the Prosecution."

"Well, then . . ."

"It just so happens," said Sloan, "that Judge Eddington is treating her refusal to plead as putting her in contempt of Court."

"If she won't play ball, then," enquired Crosby more colloquially, "how do we know where to begin?"

"At the beginning," snapped Sloan.

"If," said Crosby mutinously, "Detective Inspector Porritt couldn't spot anything wrong how are we going to?"

"I'm not sure," said Sloan with perfect truth. "Moreover," he added hastily, "there may not be anything wrong with the police case anyway. It's quite on the cards that Lucy Durmast may have perfectly good reasons of her own for keeping silent."

"Least said, soonest mended, sir," said the constable sententiously.

"That's only one of them."

"Perhaps," suggested Crosby, "she doesn't want to incriminate someone else—you know, shielding a man she loves and all that jazz."

"I have news for you, Crosby," said Sloan heavily. "There does not appear to be anyone else to incriminate."

"No one in the running at all?"

"Not as far as Inspector Porritt could see."

"Just Lucy Durmast?" The detective constable was already showing signs of losing interest.

"The deceased had lunch with her," said Sloan, adding astringently, "that, at least, does not appear to be in doubt. And he died some time afterwards from poisoning by hyoscine."

"Is that?"

"Is what?"

"Is that in doubt?" asked Crosby.

"Dr. Bressingham seemed quite sure," said Sloan drily.

The name clearly meant nothing to the detective constable.

"He's the new pathologist over in Calleford," said Sloan. "He's only been there about a year. He says he found hyoscine hydrobromide in Kenneth Carline's body in sufficient quantity to cause death."

"So we've only got his word for it?"

"His sworn word, Crosby," Sloan reminded him gently. "I believe, in fact, duplicate samples of—er—everything were also kept for any forensic pathologist retained by the Defence."

"Only there isn't one, sir? That right?"

"That's right, Crosby. You've got the general idea."

"And the old judge doesn't like the thought of no one going in to bat for the accused?"

"I couldn't have put it better myself," murmured Sloan, "although I daresay His Honour could."

The constable hitched his shoulder and said, "What are we going to do about it, then?"

"Go over the ground again," said Sloan grimly. "And again. And again."

Detective Constable Crosby groaned aloud.

It was as well for both police officers that Detective Inspector Sloan interpreted going over the ground literally. There was nothing Detective Constable Crosby enjoyed more than driving a fast car.

"Braffle Episcopi, please, Crosby," commanded Sloan presently, climbing into the front passenger seat beside the constable. Just as all good fairy tales properly begin "Once upon a time," the scene of the crime seemed the best place to start.

"Yes, sir." He slammed the car into first gear with a flourish.

"Crosby, as you yourself remarked, the trail is already quite cold. There is therefore no immediate hurry about our getting there."

"No, sir." Crosby took a corner at speed.

"But in the interests of justice, it would be helpful to get there in one piece."

"Yes, sir."

Sloan supposed that serving justice could best describe what they were doing at the moment: he couldn't think of another way of putting it except making assurance doubly sure. It was funny how clichés came into their own at times . . .

"Did she have a reason, sir?" Crosby interrupted his reverie. "A motive . . ."

"The oldest one of them all," said Sloan.

There was a pause while Crosby negotiated some road works at a pace not allowed for by the contractors: and thought about this. "Jealousy, sir?" he hazarded as the police vehicle finished executing a tight slalom round some "No Waiting" cones.

"The deceased had just announced his engagement to someone else," said Sloan. "He'd fixed it up with his fiancée over the Christmas holidays. The girl next door in his home town."

"Is that why she did for him?" asked Crosby. He hadn't travelled far in love himself and was still curious about everything to do with affairs of the heart.

"The Prosecution will say . . ." began Sloan.

"Given half a chance," put in Crosby.

"Given half a chance," agreed Sloan, "the Prosecution will say that there was some talk of Lucy Durmast having been friendly with Kenneth Carline when he first joined the firm."

"And I suppose," said Crosby, "we'll never know what the Defence would have said seeing as there isn't going to be any Defence."

"Quite so," said Sloan. "Mind you, the Prosecution agree that this talk might well only be office gossip."

"Gossipy places, offices," said Crosby, overlooking what went on in the canteen at the police station.

"But there is evidence that it was current earlier last year." Inspector Porritt had been meticulous about the inclusion of this in his report.

"No smoke without fire," said the detective constable largely.

"Smoke signals can be misread," countered Sloan. He clutched at his safety belt. "Mind that bus!"

"Plenty of room," said Crosby airily, adding with apparent detachment, "How long did Kenneth Carline take to get from Calleford to Palshaw that day?"

Detective Inspector Sloan was not deceived. "Nowhere long enough to satisfy a magistrate that he had kept to the speed limit," he said evasively, "and rather more quickly than you are going to be, Crosby."

"Yes, sir."

"That motorway is meant as road and not as race track and mind you don't forget it."

"No, sir."

Calleshire was as yet not well endowed with motorways—in fact that from Luston in the northwest of the county to Calleford more or less in the centre and thence on to Kinnisport in the east constituted its longest stretch. It was just beyond Kinnisport at the wooded waterside village of Palshaw that the motorway came out of the trees and finished in a flurry of tunnel approaches and the road itself plunged under the estuary of the river Calle. South of the river mouth the road assumed a new significance and sought its way to the coast again behind the headland, past the villages of Edsway and Braffle Episcopi beyond it to the brand-new nuclear waste disposal plant at Marby juxta Mare.

It was the nuclear waste disposal plant which had constituted the raison d'être for the tunnel in the first place. Or, rather, had been the reason for the tunnel's coming when it did. The people to the south of the estuary had been trying to persuade the Calleshire County Council to build a bridge or put in a tunnel there ever since Isambard Kingdom Brunel had demonstrated the possibilities elsewhere. A bridge had certainly been on the tapis at County Hall for the best part of fifty years. What had amazed the more naïve of the local populace, though, had been the speed with which the tunnel had been built once the nuclear waste plan had been bruited, and there had been mutterings in several quarters about back-scratching in high places.

The Action Group Against Marby had been prominent among the protesters and the most scornful about the tunnel. A quid pro quo they called it and in no way abated their opposition to the nuclear waste disposal plant. Residents south of the river had been more muted in their response. They didn't want the nuclear waste plant but they did want the tunnel and access to the motorway. The only alternative route was a slow and tediously winding road to Billing Bridge which spanned the river Calle at the widest point at which it had been possible when it was built in 1484.

"And be careful on the bends," adjured Sloan. "It was on a bend that Kenneth Carline came to grief . . ."

"I thought he was poisoned . . ."

"The theory," said Sloan, "is that the deceased dozed off at the wheel after leaving the Old Rectory."

"Drank too much lunch, did he?"

"Hyoscine hydrobromide," said Sloan repressively, "causes drowsiness."

Crosby crouched forward at the wheel to demonstrate his alertness.

Sloan said, "Carline crashed his vehicle on a bend on his way back to the tunnel at Palshaw. He was found unconscious in a hedge. The ambulance took him to Calleford Hospital where he died without coming round. That's how he fetched up on Inspector Porritt's plate."

"Sir, this hyoscine stuff . . ."

"Yes?"

"It doesn't grow on trees, does it?"

"I don't know what it grows on," said Sloan truthfully, "but if you are asking where Lucy Durmast could have got hold of some, I can tell you that."

"Where?"

"Her old grandfather was a retired general medical practitioner. He'd practised over in Luston all his working life."

"So?"

"He died last November. Lucy Durmast helped her father clear the house. Apparently the old chap had never thrown anything away—his dispensary was still full of drugs. According to Trevor Porritt's report, she could have helped herself to anything she liked."

"Proper 'Dr. Finlay's Casebook' stuff, eh?" said Crosby, whose television watching was unpredictable.

"There's another thing," said Sloan.

"Sir?"

"Hyoscine has a bitter flavour." Sloan unconsciously moistened his lips. "A sort of acrid taste."

"The pill needed sugaring, did it?"

"She served him chili con carne," said Sloan meaningfully.

"I see, sir." The detective constable caught sight of a stretch of open road at last and put his foot down. "So she had the triple alliance all right."

"What's that?" enquired Sloan when he could get his breath back.

"Like they taught us at the Training School."

"What was that?" That which Detective Constable Crosby had been taught did not, in Sloan's view, amount to a hill of beans anyway.

"The three things you need for murder, sir, the Triple Alliance."

"Tell me," invited Sloan grittily.

"Means, motive and opportunity. She'd got the lot, hadn't she?"

Cecelia Allsworthy put the telephone receiver down and went through to the kitchen of the Manor House at Braffle Episcopi. A younger girl was there folding baby clothes and keeping her eye on twin infants in a portable play-pen.

"Hortense," she said, "I'm just popping over to the Old Rectory to open it up for some—er—gentlemen."

"Mais oui, je comprends—I mean, I understand, Cecelia."

"I shan't be long." Cecelia forbore to explain that it was the police who were coming. Hortense's English was improving daily but "Your policeman are wonderful" wasn't exactly one of her stock phrases yet. "I've got the key, you see. I'm looking after the house for my friend who isn't there at the moment . . ."

"But yes . . ." said the young French girl.

"Look after Gog and Magog for me while I'm gone, won't you?" Cecelia blew the twins a kiss and let herself out of the garden door of the Manor House.

Hortense flew to the children in case they cried when their mother left them, but both little boys were entirely absorbed in tumbling about in the play-pen like porpoises. "Now, Timothee, darling, Maman won't be long, and Michael . . ." Hortense could —just—understand Cecelia's preoccupation with pottery design and production. She would never understand how it was that she could refer to her two beautiful babies as Gog and Magog. The English were indeed a heartless race.

Cecelia Allsworthy slipped across the Manor House lawn and through their private gate into the churchyard. The Old Rectory was situated right round the other side of the church. These days Braffle Episcopi shared a rector with two neighbouring villages and the rectory had been sold off by the ecclesiastical authorities. As she crunched her way over the church path towards the closed door, Cecelia reflected sadly on how often it had been open to her. She didn't like seeing the house shut up.

She slipped her key under the guard and into the lock. She didn't enjoy going into the house any more either. It wasn't the same empty of Durmasts: without Lucy's giving a smile of welcome as she entered, Cecelia felt estranged. She gave herself a tiny shake and reminded herself that no house was the same if there weren't people living in it. She decided that what the Old Rectory needed was fresh air and went into several rooms, flinging the windows wide open.

That done, she gravitated towards the kitchen simply because this was what she had always done. Lucy was a good cook and enjoyed practising the culinary arts in the same way as Cecelia enjoyed making pottery—she stopped her train of thought. No, that wasn't strictly true. Lucy didn't feel as passionately about cooking as Cecelia did about pottery. She might do it well—she'd jolly well had to become a good cook on account of her mother dying young—but she didn't feel the same way about handling ingredients as Cecelia did about taking clay and forming it into something beautiful. Cecelia's elemental struggle with shape was something she couldn't convey in words—not even to a sympathetic husband or understanding friend. Only her artistic peers comprehended some of her feelings.

She pulled herself up short in the middle of the kitchen. She should be thinking about Lucy, not about herself, and yet she was aware that there was nothing more she could run through her mind about Lucy that hadn't already been through it a hundred times and more. She had exhausted herself over Kenneth Carline's death and Lucy's arrest long ago and knew she had nothing to add any more.

Presently she found herself saying just this to Detective Inspector Sloan.

"I quite understand," he said, "but if we might see the house I think it would help me to—er—envisage what might have happened."

"Then you're a better man than I am," said Cecelia Allsworthy flatly, "because I've tried and I can't. Not Lucy of all people."

Detective Inspector Sloan nodded. It was a refrain he heard almost every time there was an arrest. No family or friend or colleague could ever imagine someone they knew doing something wrong. And the better they knew them the more difficult it became for them to understand. It was as if the fact of knowing another human being well threw a mantle of goodness over them.

Detective Constable Crosby was apparently not troubled by thoughts of any kind. "Nice place they've got here, haven't they?" he said generally.

Cecelia Allsworthy nodded. "It's early eighteenth century." The Manor House was older by a hundred years and more. "The parson lived in style then and had a big family into the bargain."

"Your friends been here long, then?" asked the constable, looking round at the furnishings.

She frowned. "Lucy's father bought it just after his firm got the

Palshaw Tunnel contract. That's about three or four years ago now. He'd been wanting to move at the time away from Calleford and this happened to be on the market."

"Mr. Durmast would have wanted to be near the workings anyway, I suppose," said Sloan.

"He used to say"—she smiled gravely—"that if he lived somewhere on the far side of the river he would have a vested interest in getting the tunnel finished on time, and it was."

Sloan reciprocated her smile with a quick one of his own and, terrierlike, came back to the point. "We're not getting a lot of cooperation from Miss Durmast," he said.

"She's got a mind of her own," said Cecelia Allsworthy. "I know she's been a bit—well, caught up—with looking after her father and all that, but it doesn't mean she can't think for herself."

"We wouldn't know about that, madam, because so far she hasn't seen fit to tell us anything."

"Nor me," said Cecelia almost cheerfully, "but you can take it from me that she's not silly."

"It wasn't a silly murder," said Sloan solemnly. "Kenneth Carline might easily have hit another car and his death been taken for a road traffic accident."

"I would have said," responded the young woman with spirit, "that whatever action Lucy takes she knows what she's doing. You can count on that."

"You weren't here the day Kenneth Carline came to lunch," said Sloan.

"Oh yes, I was," said Cecelia Allsworthy unexpectedly. "I'd come over for morning coffee after I'd got the twins ready—it was too cold for a long walk and Lucy's kitchen is—was—always lovely and warm. They've got one of those big ranges that never goes out —unless you want it to, of course. Come through and see."

Nothing loath, the two policemen trooped after her into the kitchen.

Cecelia put her hand on the kitchen range. "It's cold now, of course."

"Of course, madam," said Sloan.

"I let it out when . . . after . . ." For the first time her voice faltered.

"Quite right, madam." It was the mundane aspects of crime that were sometimes as harrowing as the violent.

A dead stove and a dead man.

Both were stone cold now.

"I used to come over most mornings then," said Cecelia more matter-of-factly, "to see Lucy and have a chat. I didn't have an *au pair* girl in those days so I couldn't get back to work anyway. Besides, the twins were younger. If," she said with an attempt at lightness, "you measure the time between an arrest and a trial it comes to about an inch of baby."

"Yes, madam, I'm sure." He cleared his throat. "That morning . . ."

"I told the other inspector all about that morning . . ."

Sloan explained what had happened to Inspector Porritt.

Mrs. Allsworthy came from a background where injuries to policemen were not considered a good thing. "I'm sorry," she said simply. "Well, it was all quite unexpected. I swear that Lucy didn't know Kenneth was coming until he telephoned."

"Kenneth?" interposed Sloan alertly. "You knew him, then?"

"I'd met him here and I'd heard her talk about him. Her father always had the new young men in the firm out to dinner and Lucy had got to know him quite well. He was a bit lonely, I think. This was his first big job away from home."

"He came from the North of England," supplied Sloan.

"And from somewhere where they played Rugby," said Cecelia. "Lucy said that that was his big thing."

Sloan came back to the day Kenneth Carline died.

"We'd finished our coffee," she said, "and I was talking about getting back and feeding Timothy and Michael when the phone rang." Celia pointed to a wall-mounted instrument. "Lucy answered it here. I heard her."

"Go on."

"She said 'Hullo, Kenneth' and then 'Of course you can. Everything you want will be in the study. As long as you know what you want you can come along and help yourself.' Then there was a bit of silence while he said something—I couldn't hear what—and then . . ."

"And then?"

Cecelia swallowed visibly. "And then Lucy said 'If you're coming all this way why don't you stay for a bite of lunch?' He said something else and then she said 'Of course, I'm sure. It's no trouble at all. I'll expect you about one o'clock, then.' "

A little silence fell in the kitchen at this point.

"That's all," finished Cecelia lamely. "And look where it's led to."

"She didn't press him particularly?"

"She didn't have to."

"What time would this have been?"

"When he rang, you mean? It was just before twelve o'clock. I remember exactly because Lucy said to me 'That's a tall order, isn't it? A hot lunch on a cold day for a hungry man and only an hour to cook it in.' "

Sloan nodded. Policemen's wives had to get used to the opposite. A hot meal for a hungry man who, irrespective of the weather, didn't come in in an hour or two or three.

Cecelia went on. "I said something silly like 'Look on it as a challenge.' "

"It sounds as if she might have done," commented Detective Constable Crosby mordantly. He was examining a spice rack on the wall.

"I remember her saying," said Cecelia, ignoring this, " 'The meat'll have to come out of a tin, that's for sure. There's no time for any shopping.' "

Sloan looked round the well-appointed kitchen. Mother Hubbard's cupboard was bare, but he doubted if Lucy Durmast's had been.

"Inspector . . ." Cecelia Allsworthy had suddenly become quite tentative.

"Yes?"

"The police searched this house afterwards . . ."

"Yes."

"Did they find . . . anything?"

"No." Sloan cleared his throat and hoped he wasn't breaking the Official Secrets Acts.

"But it doesn't signify, I suppose?" Cecelia's shoulders drooped.

"Kenneth Carline didn't die straightaway," said Sloan.

"So she would have had time . . ."

"All the time in the world."

SIX

Pigmenta—Paints

Ronald and Phyllis Bolsover made no bones about seeing the police yet again.

"We quite understand the difficulties, Inspector," said the deputy chairman of William Durmast Ltd., Civil Engineers. "We—my wife and I, that is—are also naturally very concerned about Lucy's position and would want to help in any way we could."

The Bolsovers lived in a smallish detached house on the outskirts of Calleford. A large Victorian-style conservatory had been added to the sunny side of the house. As they had approached the front door, Sloan had caught sight of a promising chiaroscuro of light and shade through the glass and even at a distance the flowers of one or two exotic plants. Now that the two policemen were in the sitting room, he had a better view of it still through the glass doors which led into the conservatory. Roses were his own favourite plant but he was prepared to be broadminded about the enthusiasms of other gardeners.

"We feel so helpless," chimed in Mrs. Bolsover. "There doesn't seem to be anything that we can do."

Sloan agreed that inaction was always difficult.

"What with her father being abroad and everything," said Phyllis Bolsover.

"He'd only just gone overseas," amplified Ronald Bolsover, "before all this happened."

"Bill had wanted to go earlier," said the woman, "but he couldn't get away because of the tunnel opening ceremony. He left straight away afterwards."

Sloan nodded his understanding. At the end of every civil-engineering construction someone cut a ribbon. It was no less a ritual in its way than the performing of a tribal dance. He wondered how the new town in Africa would celebrate its completion.

"The Minister of Transport himself," explained Bolsover with modest pride, "came down to perform the ceremony. There's a plaque."

"I think I remember some photographs in the newspaper," began Sloan.

A shadow crossed Bolsover's face. "It was a pity about the demonstration," he said.

"Happens all the time," said the police inspector philosophically.

"It was the Action Against Marby Group," said Ronald Bolsover. "They've been against the nuclear waste plant there right from the beginning and saw their chance to get some extra publicity."

"Which they did," said Phyllis Bolsover astringently. She was a rather faded woman with neat features and must have been quite pretty once.

"They managed to get a banner right over the tunnel mouth," said Bolsover. "Lowered it just as the Minister arrived. Far too late for us to do anything about it." He winced at the recollection. "It said MARBY CAN SERIOUSLY DAMAGE YOUR HEALTH."

"You could hardly see the entrance," said Mrs. Bolsover. "It was a shame."

"I'm afraid that's true, Inspector," agreed Ronald Bolsover. "It was most unfortunate from a publicity point of view. All that the press wanted to do was to focus on the activists."

Sloan agreed that publicity could sometimes misfire badly.

"Misfire!" exploded the deputy chairman. "I'll say it misfired. The reporters weren't interested in either the Minister or the tunnel. They practically ignored our press handout and concentrated on the Marby lot instead."

"Mrs. Othen," contributed Phyllis Bolsover, "said that her husband was most upset too. I was standing next to her."

"Eric Othen," explained Bolsover unnecessarily, "is the County Surveyor."

Sloan nodded. The name of Eric Othen was on all the paperwork from County Hall that concerned the constabulary and the road network of the county of Calleshire, and was thus well known to all policemen.

"And I'm not surprised that Othen was upset," continued Bolsover. "I've never heard such a load of nonsense as the Action Group gave the reporter. Melissa Wainwright—that's their leader —went on at him for ages. What she knows about how a nuclear waste plant functions would go on a sixpence. The fool lapped it up, too, and the next day it was all in the papers. They hardly mentioned the tunnel."

"Disappointing for you, sir," said Sloan. The Calleshire County Constabulary didn't have an official view on Nuclear Waste Disposal Plants: only on demonstrations for or against them. It was sometimes too subtle a distinction for the policemen who lost their helmets in the mêlée.

"I know the Minister felt it badly," said Bolsover.

"Politicians tend to take things personally." Sloan was not unsympathetic. "They never know what's going to backfire, of course."

Bolsover gave a thin smile. "I must say I'd rather be a civil engineer myself. You know where you are with materials and machinery. They always behave in the same way."

"Yes, sir, that's very true." Sloan pulled out Inspector Porritt's report. "Men aren't so consistent, are they?"

"Give me steel and concrete," Bolsover said fervently, "and I'll make something of it for you."

There was something less tangible that Sloan didn't quite know what to make of. "You say Mr. Durmast left the country as soon as the tunnel had been officially opened?"

The civil engineer nodded. "He'd been out in Dlasa last year seeing to the preliminaries of Mgongwala. Working on site selection and so forth. There had to be some feasibility studies on soil suitability and transport and water supplies and so forth before the actual work began."

Sloan wondered if the Pyramids had begun that way.

Or Stonehenge.

"But," went on Bolsover, "in January as soon as the official opening of the tunnel was over Bill went out to Dlasa again to get the job started properly."

"Before . . ."

"Before Kenneth Carline died." Bolsover frowned. "And he's not due back for quite a while. We get reports in the office, of course, and all I can say is that just now the project is at a very delicate and important stage in its development."

"And his daughter would know this?"

"Very much so." He was emphatic about this. "Bill was always a man who took his work home with him."

Sloan nodded. Some policemen did and some didn't. Sometimes the human burden needed unloading onto wifely ears. Sometimes, though, it concerned matters better left unshared . . .

"Literally, too," expanded Bolsover. "I mean he did a lot of design work in the Old Rectory as well. He said he could work better there than in the office."

Detective Inspector Sloan tapped the report on his knee and came back to the subject that they'd been skirting around. "There are just one or two things I'd like to get quite straight about the day Kenneth Carline died."

"Of course." Bolsover turned and faced Sloan, his back to the conservatory doors. Beyond him the foliage of a giant Begonia Rex positively burgeoned. "I've been over it again and again in my mind, naturally."

"Naturally," said Detective Constable Crosby for no reason at all.

"Carline came to see me in my office," said Bolsover.

"When exactly?" asked Sloan, conscious of an obscure need to resume the initiative.

"About eleven o'clock in the morning."

"What did he come to see you about?"

"The breakdown of some figures that a firm of quantity surveyors were waiting for." Bolsover waved a hand. "We're doing a job over at the airport at the moment."

"The runway extension?" Sloan knew that there was work going on at Malperton—Calleshire's tiny neighbourhood airport.

"None other." He grimaced. "It's not exactly a gripping roast compared with a tunnel and a new town but it's good bread-and-butter work all the same. We concentrated on the figures for about an hour and then I told Carline that I had another job for him."

Sloan looked up enquiringly.

"I needed him as my assistant that afternoon," said Bolsover. "At the Palshaw Tunnel. The last of the retention fee was due to be handed over to the contractors and I'd arranged to make my final on-site inspection at two o'clock that day."

"I see, sir." This was old hat to Sloan, who had read it all in Inspector Porritt's report, but there was no harm in hearing it again.

"I asked Carline to call at the Old Rectory first to pick up Bill's original drawings for me to look at again," said Bolsover. "I wanted to be on the safe side before I signed on the dotted line."

"Quite so, sir."

"And then I told him to meet me at the Palshaw end of the tunnel at two o'clock. Only he didn't come."

A small silence fell in the Bolsover drawing room.

It was Crosby who broke it. "Gone to join the great majority, hadn't he?"

When Lucy Durmast had been a little girl at school she had gone through the same phases as all her friends as they came to grips with the meaning of words and the understanding of parts of speech. Trick questions were the order of the day. One which had gone the rounds had been the hoary old chestnut "Constantinople is a long word. How do you spell it?" to which the answer of the initiated was "I T." (The father, though, who answered his daughter's "Daddy, I'm hot" with "Hello Hot, I'm Daddy" was generally felt to be not playing the game.)

Another popular question had been "What is the longest word in the English language?"

Lucy had known the answer to that quite early on.

Antidisestablishmentarianism.

At the age of eleven going on twelve she had known the word but not what it meant.

At the age of twenty-one going on twenty-two she now not only knew its meaning but was beginning to have a firm opinion on the subject itself.

This had been provoked by a visit from the prison chaplain. She hadn't needed to see him if she hadn't wanted to. He had made that perfectly clear. Lucy had discovered to her own total surprise, though, that she had wanted to see him quite badly and she had found herself nodding her assent when she had instead really meant to shake her head when he asked.

Until she met the Reverend George Conway, Lucy Durmast's knowledge of prison chaplains had been confined to the solitary reference in Oscar Wilde's "The Ballad of Reading Gaol":

> And twice a day the Chaplain called
> And left a little tract.

This clergyman had nothing in his hands when he came to see her.

"Lucy Durmast?" he said, standing before her. "I'm George Conway. May I sit down?"

She nodded.

He was a neat, spare man, who somehow contrived to create a feeling of space about him, bringing dignity and grace to distinctly unpromising surroundings. Over the years he had developed an all-purpose opening gambit with his disparate flock. "How are you getting along?" he asked generally. "Managing?"

She opened her hands in an age-old gesture of despair that needed no words.

"All bad things come to an end, you know," he said gently. "Just like all good things. Don't forget that." He gave her a quick smile. "There is always a light at the end of the tunnel and whatever you may think, it isn't necessarily a train coming the other way."

She managed a half smile.

"Well done," he said. A half smile might not amount to much in the outside world. In a prison setting it was worth a great deal, and George Conway was quick to acknowledge this. "Letters getting through all right?"

She nodded. Cecelia Allsworthy had written faithfully, saying nothing but conveying much love and affection.

"And visitors?"

She shook her head so violently that the chaplain quite mistook her meaning.

"Problems?" he said quickly. "Do you want me to . . . oh, I see. You don't want any visitors. I understand . . ." This was something he did comprehend too. Those there would always be who didn't want to be seen in prison by their friends and family.

Lucy's agitation subsided.

"Would you," he asked diffidently, "like to talk to me about it?" In his time he had sat and listened to both bared souls and barefaced lying with the same expression of alert interest and total absence of condemnation, utterly confident in the power of his Creator to love saint and sinner alike.

She looked at him, carefully weighing the situation. What she didn't know was where Church and State overlapped. Antidisestablishmentarianism might well be the longest word in the English language but it didn't help a lot at this particular moment. What she wanted to know was exactly where the Reverend George Conway's allegiance lay. Was it with the Home Secretary or with His Grace the Bishop of Calleford?

Or both?

The Chaplain said, "Don't feel you have to, of course."

No man can serve two masters, thought Lucy, even if they're both establishment figures.

"Burdens," continued the chaplain matter-of-factly, "are usually easier shared."

Something from *The Pilgrim's Progress* flashed through her mind: Christian had carried a burden, hadn't he? Surely, though, his burden hadn't slipped from him until the very end of his journey. Unconsciously she gave a little shiver and her shoulders sagged.

"Sometimes," persisted George Conway, missing neither sign, "even just talking to someone helps."

She nodded. She was finding it very difficult to think straight with him sitting opposite her, projecting humanity and compassion. What she needed to know was whether or not he had obligations to Caesar. Did he have to walk a delicate tightrope between Church and State? Look at poor Sir Thomas More . . .

"Sometimes, though," said the Chaplain equably, "people get by more easily by just taking one day at a time."

Something inside her wanted to say "Sufficient unto the say is the evil thereof" but she didn't allow the words to pass her lips. Anyway you weren't supposed to quote the Bible at clergymen: it was role reversal or something.

"I'm sure that's all we're meant to do," he went on with conviction.

Oddly enough it was his use of the plural pronoun "we" that registered with Lucy at that moment. Prison was a place of "us" and "them": not "we." The chaplain was doing what he could to restore her to the human race . . .

"And you, I hear," he said lightly, "have taken some sort of unofficial vow of silence."

There was no mistaking her assent to that. She'd grinned before she could help herself.

"Confounding all and sundry, I'm sure," he said.

She hung her head in mock penitence. They must have made an incongruous pair, thought Lucy, with a sudden flash of genuine humour. She wondered what an artist would have made of them as a subject. The prisoner and the clergymen—a conversation piece.

Except that in another sense there hadn't been any conversation. There had been communication though.

The Reverend George Conway said cheerfully, "I shouldn't worry too much about that if I were you."

She looked up.

"You can't," he said, "be half as troublesome a prisoner as St. Paul was."

Her smile was sudden and spontaneous. She had forgotten that St. Paul had been in prison too.

"And he didn't keep quiet either," said the chaplain. "A most articulate man, St. Paul."

The prisoner who oddly enough had been in Lucy's mind most of all had been Napoleon Bonaparte. That, too, stemmed from a childhood memory of word games at school. After the longest word in the English language had come the longest palindrome. "Able was I ere I saw Elba" was ingrained in every schoolchild's mind. The phrase had come back to her one night and summed up her own feelings so neatly that she hadn't been able to get it out of her mind. She had never in a hundred years expected to feel any empathy with the French Emperor but she did now.

The chaplain got up to go. "By the way," he said, "there is something that St. Paul said that you mustn't ever forget."

She looked at him.

"That nothing shall be able to separate us from the love of God." He lifted a hand in benediction and said, "God bless you, my child . . ."

Suddenly overcome, Lucy Durmast was really and truly without words at that moment. She would have found them now if she could. She struggled to speak, but by the time she was able to do so the chaplain had gone.

Crosby hunched his shoulders as they left the Bolsovers' house. "Open and shut, if you ask me, sir."

Sloan nodded reflectively. "I suppose you could say that Inspector Porritt had got everything buttoned up except the girl's statement."

"You can play your cards so close to your chest that they fall down your shirt," said the constable graphically.

Sloan didn't say anything.

"And you don't have to help the police with their enquiries either," sniffed Crosby. "It's a free country."

"True," agreed Sloan. Exercising the right of lawful protest came in there somewhere.

"In America," Crosby informed him, "they stand on the Fifth Amendment."

"You don't say," murmured Sloan. Crosby was an aficionado of the silver screen and thus well informed on the American Constitution.

"Plead that," said the constable, "and you don't have to say a thing."

"It is a cardinal principle of English law, too," Sloan reminded him, "that you don't have to say anything that might incriminate yourself."

"Well, then . . ."

"But if you stay silent," pointed out Sloan, "everyone is entitled to draw their own conclusions from that silence."

"So all we've got to go on, sir, is evidence? Is that right?"

"It is," said Sloan cautiously, suspecting irony somewhere.

"Well, then . . ."

Eminent authorities on jurisprudence, conceded Sloan silently, might take longer to reach the same conclusion, but it stood.

"And there isn't any contrary evidence?" asked Crosby. "Nothing to show she might be innocent?"

Sloan considered this carefully. Actually there had been something that niggled, something that didn't quite tie up. "There's a list of things that Inspector Porritt found in the deceased's car afterwards."

"The tunnel plans?"

"Those," agreed Sloan, "and something else."

Crosby stood still and waited, his hand on the police car door.

"Some leaflets," said Sloan, "protesting about the nuclear waste plant at Marby."

SEVEN

Nebulae—Sprays

None of Kenneth Carline's flat-mates had the look of nuclear protesters. The two policemen saw them that evening after work at
their dwelling place—a portion of a large old house in Calleford
long ago divided up into flats. The owner lived on the ground floor
and acted as concierge. Gerry Porteous, who answered the door,
was a short-back-and-sides man and gave his occupation as trainee
accountant.

"We come old, Inspector," he said, "because it's a long training."

Sloan nodded. He himself was old enough now to find age relative.

Alan Marshall, it transpired, worked for the Calleford office of
an extremely superior firm of land agents and surveyors, and Colin
Jervis, the third man there, for a bank. All three were sturdily built
and, if the scattered accoutrements of various games were anything
to go by, were more devoted to sport than to politics.

Another pointer to their interest in things non-political was that
the mention of the word "police" did not arouse noticeably strong
reactions. Nobody shouted anything offensive—indeed, Alan Marshall actually pushed a chair forward for Sloan.

"We're just going over one or two things again before the trial,"
said Sloan generally.

Three young men waited attentively for him to go on.

"You might have had some further thoughts too," said Sloan.

Porteous for one shook his head.

"You never know," remarked Crosby from the sidelines.

"There isn't anything we haven't thought of," said Porteous
heavily.

"It was worth an ask," said Crosby.

Sloan didn't say anything. A man could only be young once but he could be immature forever.

Alan Marshall stirred. "Anyway, Inspector, we told the other policeman everything."

"Not that there was a lot to tell." Colin Jervis shrugged his shoulders expressively. "It was just an ordinary weekend for us."

"The only thing that was different . . ." began Porteous.

"Yes?" said Sloan. It was part of his own professional calling that he was interested in any change in a pattern.

Gerry Porteous said, "The only thing that was different was that Ken didn't go to the Kipper Club with the others."

"Kipper Club?" said Sloan swiftly.

"It's a tradition that the team meets for a late breakfast every Sunday morning after the match," said Porteous.

"We have kippers," expanded Marshall helpfully.

Jervis, too, seemed to think some gilding of the lily was called for. "It works as a sort of roll call for the fifteen after Saturday night."

"And Carline didn't come that last Sunday?" asked Sloan patiently.

"That's right," said Porteous. "He said he was too bruised."

"He'd got a real bashing in the game on the Saturday, you see," said Jervis.

"Some beggar seemed to have it in for him all right," said Porteous.

"Mind you," said Jervis, "Luston play rough at the best of times."

"Needle match, of course," observed Marshall. "I suppose you could call it a sort of local Derby."

This wasn't news to Sloan or Crosby. Policemen from Berebury were regularly drafted to the stadium at Luston on Saturday afternoons for crowd duty.

"A marked man, that's what he said he was," weighed in Marshall.

Policing a stadium was an analogy dear to the heart of lecturers at the Cadet Training College. The perfect example, it was said, of the measured need for policemen, was a football stadium. Empty and one policeman could take care of it: full of spectators and four hundred couldn't.

"And he was so rotten on the Sunday morning after the match

that he didn't go to the Kipper Club?" Sloan hoped he'd sorted this out at last.

Three men nodded.

"But all right by Monday morning, though?" persisted Sloan.

"Nearly all right," said Gerry Porteous.

"He looked a bit of a mess," said Marshall.

"Two lovely black eyes?" suggested Sloan crisply.

"More of a cauliflower ear," said Marshall.

"He must have been on the ref's blind side all afternoon," said Porteous.

Detective Constable Crosby's wayward interest was aroused at last. "Where was he in the scrum?"

"Middle row."

"Dangerous place," remarked Crosby.

"Not as dangerous," said Marshall soberly, "as lunch with a lady."

"True," said Crosby.

In his mind Sloan likened middle row forward on the Rugby field to the second row in a police line of defence against a crowd. The front row, arms linked, took the brunt, but when the set scrum collapsed, so to speak, the greater danger fell to the second row. What came out of the maul when the contest was the Police Force versus the Mob was usually injuries.

Demonstrations reminded Sloan of something else.

Was Carline, he asked all the young men, caught up at all with the nuclear waste disposal plant at Marby juxta Mare?

Gerry Porteous frowned. "Did the noble firm of William Durmast build that? I don't think they did."

"I'm pretty sure," said Marshall, "that Ken once said that the atomic-energy authorities had some specialist construction people down for Marby."

"Not everyone's cup of tea," contributed Jervis, "atomic waste."

"Horses for course," said Crosby.

Sloan explained that he hadn't meant that. Had Carline been an activist in nuclear protesting? he asked.

Three young men shook their heads.

"Not his scene at all," said Colin Jervis emphatically.

"He was against politics anyway," said Gerry Porteous somewhat naïvely.

Detective Inspector Sloan was not sufficiently exalted in rank to attend meetings of the Berebury Watch Committee let alone those of the Calleshire Police Committee, but he knew that, like the poor, politics were always there.

"Especially African ones," added Porteous.

Sloan lifted an eyebrow.

"Ken had had to do some of the groundwork calculations for this new town in Africa that his firm are building," explained Porteous. "The preliminary brief for the quantity surveyors and so forth."

"Well?"

"Politics came into that."

Sloan could well believe it.

"It was the missionaries really," said Alan Marshall. "Ken told us all about it."

Sloan nodded. Politics and religion were hard forces to harness. Many a world leader had found that out for himself.

Colin Jervis said, "Blow me if some missionaries hadn't delivered a load of mattocks to Dlasa for ground clearance without so much as a by-your-leave."

"Not a good thing?" hazarded Sloan.

"Completely upset the local economy," pronounced Colin Jervis with all the authority of one who worked in a bank.

"How?" enquired Sloan warily. Economics were a closed book to him. They constituted a strange, illogical territory where two and two didn't always make four, where success in production was nearly as hazardous as failure.

"In Dlasa," explained Jervis, "the bride-price was paid in mattocks."

"I see," said Sloan. He'd heard somewhere that the questions in economics examination papers stayed the same from year to year and it was the correct answers that changed. He could well believe it.

"With an excess of mattocks," said Jervis, "the barter system broke down."

"Mattocks," chimed in Gerry Porteous, "being a sort of currency."

"And it had been devalued?" asked Sloan. Devaluing the currency was a crime in a class of its own: one that Sloan did understand. He and his wife Margaret, had once been taken on a guided tour of a ruined Scottish castle. The curator had waxed eloquent

on the iniquities of the wicked earl who had owned it in the six-
teenth century and reeled off a positive Newgate Calendar list of
his crimes. Murder, rapine, pillage, blackmail and abduction had
been made to seem very run-of-the-mill by the curator, who had
been working his way up to a dramatic climax. With lowered voice
he had finished on a high note, "And he even fiddled the currency,
too."

"The brides," said Porteous solemnly, "didn't know what to do,
with mattocks being two a penny after that."

"Very upsetting," agreed Sloan.

"Ken didn't know what to do either," said Marshall, "with the
local economy all haywire. It upset all his calculations."

Sloan nodded his sympathy. Politics, religion and economics
were an even more heady trio to mix. Bride-prices, though, reminded him of something else. He said "Lucy Durmast . . ."

There was a perceptible stiffening all round.

"Nothing in it on Ken's side," affirmed Porteous.

"All right," conceded Marshall, "he took her out once or twice.
And he went there quite a lot. His boss liked working at home and
they did a lot of eating at the Old Rectory after work."

"Just good friends?" suggested Crosby from the sidelines.

"Girls get funny ideas," said the trainee accountant seriously.
"You've got to be careful."

"Perhaps Carline wasn't careful enough," hazarded Sloan, wondering if accountancy and caution always went hand in hand.

"Hell hath no fury like a woman scorned," said Colin Jervis
sagely.

"Did she come here?" asked Sloan.

Three young men shook their heads in unison.

"Never?"

"Never," said Gerry Porteous.

"The landlady doesn't allow girls over the threshold," explained
Jervis.

That explained the male ménage. "Old-fashioned?" said Sloan.

"She's got two daughters she can't marry off," said Marshall
bitterly.

"And no wonder," said Jervis.

"Did Carline have any visitors at all?" asked Sloan routinely.

There was a reaction to this of a different kind: it was more
difficult to define, but the policeman was immediately aware of it.

"Occasionally," said Gerry Porteous with noticeable wariness.

"Anyone in particular?" asked Sloan casually.

"A chap called Aturu came a few times," said Porteous equally casually.

"Not an Englishman," remarked Sloan.

"That's true," agreed Porteous as if the thought were a new one.

"A fellow Ken was at college with," explained Jervis.

"I see," said Sloan evenly. "An old friend, you might say?"

"Sort of . . ." Jervis cleared his throat.

"This Mr. Aturu . . ." began Sloan.

"Actually, Inspector," Porteous interrupted him awkwardly, "he's not Mr. Aturu."

"Oh?"

It was Colin Jervis who plunged into the conversational lacuna that had been created. "He's Prince Aturu."

"Is he?" said Sloan softly. "And who's he when he's at home?"

"One of the sons of King Thabile III of Dlasa," said Jervis unhappily.

"I don't like it, Sloan," declared Superintendent Leeyes predictably.

"No, sir."

"One of the King's sons, you said."

"Yes, sir."

"But not—ah—one of the King's men?"

"No, sir."

"Getting involved with a junior member of the construction firm that's building a palace for his father."

"Capital city . . ."

"Same thing."

Detective Inspector Sloan knew better than to argue. "They were at college together," he said instead. "Kenneth Carline and Prince Aturu."

"Perhaps that's how Durmast's got the contract," suggested Leeyes, who was always deeply suspicious of the old school tie.

"No, sir, I don't think so." Sloan took a deep breath. "You see, Prince Aturu is against the building of the new capital city at Mgongwala."

"Sons," pronounced Leeyes sagely, "have always opposed fathers."

"Actively against . . ."

"Since Adam and Cain and Abel," continued Leeyes. "It's in the nature of things."

"Prince Aturu," remarked Sloan with apparent inconsequence, "is in this country doing a post-graduate degree in economics."

Superintendent Leeyes glared at him and said that that didn't alter the father-and-son relationship, or did it?

"The Prince," observed Sloan neutrally, "feels that a new city is going to be bad for Dlasa."

"Very probably," said Leeyes.

"Very bad," said Sloan.

"But good for William Durmast, Civil Engineers."

"The Prince's argument," reported Sloan, who had abstracted it from Gerry Porteous, who had heard it from Kenneth Carline, "was that conspicuous expenditure didn't do anything for the French royal family."

"They had a revolution," said Leeyes succinctly.

"Quite so," said Sloan.

"A lot of *avoir la tête tranchée,*" said Leeyes in atrocious French. He had once attended an evening class course in French conversation: the lecturer had been heard to declare that he would have preferred to have had Winston Churchill in it: his accent had been better. "*À la lanterne* and all that, Sloan."

Detective Inspector Sloan did not know if there were "To the barricades" touches in modern Dlasa. Or, if there were, if it was anything to do with the Calleshire Police Force.

"I don't like it," repeated Leeyes.

"No, sir."

"What," he enquired, "did Inspector Porritt have to say about this dissident son?"

Sloan tightened his lips. "I'm afraid he wasn't told very much, sir. Only that an old college friend of the deceased had been trying to get in touch. That's all."

"Not that he was Dlasian?"

"No, sir. Carline's flatmates didn't think it was important."

"That's for us to judge," said Leeyes magisterially.

Sloan nodded. Doctors took the same view about symptoms. Patients weren't the best judges of those. What mattered to the patient and what mattered to the doctor were two different things. Theirs to do and die . . . no, that was something else.

"When?" The superintendent's voice broke into this reverie.

"When what, sir?" Sloan asked, startled.

"When did this Prince Aturu try to get in touch?" snapped Leeyes impatiently. "In relation to the death."

"He telephoned the flat the following Monday after Carline died. A week later, that is. Apparently he'd had a date with Carline at the weekend and, of course, the deceased had not appeared . . ." On second thought he could perhaps have put that more felicitously.

Leeyes grunted.

"According to Gerry Porteous—that's the man there he spoke to —Prince Aturu hadn't heard about the death . . ."

"Murder," said Leeyes flatly.

"Murder," amended Sloan, "and was very surprised and upset about it when Porteous told him."

Leeyes sniffed. "He was, was he?"

"The deceased's friends," said Sloan carefully, "were of the opinion that Kenneth was—er—having to dance pretty with the Prince."

"Divided loyalties come difficult," pronounced Leeyes.

"I should have thought," said Detective Inspector Sloan, family man and mortgagee, "that he ought to have known which side his bread was buttered on."

"Perhaps he did," said Leeyes chillingly.

"Gerry Porteous knew," said Detective Inspector Sloan. "He told me that he warned Carline to be careful about what he said to the Prince." Economics might be a new science but accountancy was an old, old one. Even trainee accountants could add.

Leeyes frowned. "Did his employers know of his connection with the King of Dlasa's son?"

Sloan was guarded. "His flatmates thought not but they weren't sure."

"You'd better find out, Sloan, to be on the safe side."

"Yes, sir."

"And see the Marby mob."

"Yes, sir." The superintendent could never bring himself to use their full title of the Marby juxta Mare Atomic Waste Disposal Plant Action Group.

"You'll have to talk to Melissa Wainwright, Sloan, you realise that, don't you?"

"Yes, sir," said Sloan without enthusiasm. Melissa Wainwright was the leading light of all the nuclear protests in Calleshire. She was a skilled campaigner, veteran of many a confrontation with the law, and no lover of the police force. The feeling, as far as Sloan was concerned, was reciprocal.

"Sergeant Watkinson," remarked Leeyes, "is out of hospital now."

"Good," said Sloan. The demonstration at the opening ceremony of the Palshaw Tunnel hadn't been peaceful.

"But still limping."

Sloan cleared his throat. "The deceased's friends say that Carline had never talked to them about nuclear disarmament or anything like that."

"But the protesters' leaflets were in his car?"

"Oh yes, sir."

Leeyes grunted. "Funny, that. Better look into it."

"Yes, sir."

"And, Sloan . . ."

"Sir?"

"When you see the pathologist over at Calleford—what did you say his name was?"

"Dr. Bressingham . . ."

"You'd better ask him if he checked for blowpipe dart marks."

"Sir?"

"You can't be too careful in this game," said Leeyes trenchantly.

EIGHT

Injectiones—Injections

"Dart marks?" echoed Dr. Bressingham a little while later. He was sitting in the office attached to his mortuary at Calleford District General Hospital. Detective Inspector Sloan and Detective Constable Crosby were sitting opposite him.

"Blowpipe dart marks," expanded Detective Constable Crosby, to whom this aspect of the investigation had instantly appealed. "Were there any on the murdered man?"

"None that I observed," replied Dr. Bressingham stiffly. He was young and rather concerned with his public image.

"Or arrow ones?"

"Arrows?" The pathologist stared at him.

"The arrows that aren't darts," amplified Crosby.

This confounded the doctor completely.

Nor did Crosby's attempt at explanation clarify anything as far as Dr. Bressingham was concerned. "Not 'the Rose and Crown' sort of darts that are called arrows, Doctor," he said, "but . . ."

"Inspector . . ." protested the pathologist.

"But the arrows that are bows and arrows," finished Crosby triumphantly.

"There were no marks on the body of the deceased from arrows either," said Dr. Bressingham coldly. He had a short beard which curiously served to make him look younger than his years. He added, "Arrows of any variety, that is."

"What about poisoned spears?" enquired Crosby with genuine interest. These had been a feature of many a comic paper of his childhood.

"I don't think," said Detective Inspector Sloan repressively, "that we need worry too much about poisoned spears." He explained the nature of their errand to the pathologist. "It's a purely routine follow-up, Doctor, because of the unfortunate accident to the officer originally involved in the enquiries into the death of Kenneth Carline."

"I performed the usual superficial examination before proceeding to the internal one," nodded Dr. Bressingham, unsmiling, "and found nothing to suggest the use of blowpipe darts, arrows or poisoned spears."

"Thank you, Doctor, that is most useful to know," said Sloan warmly, perjuring his immortal soul in a good cause.

"Furthermore," added the pathologist, "nor did I find any injection sites."

It was Sloan's turn to nod. There were fashions in plagues. At least Kenneth Carline hadn't been into drugs.

"You must appreciate, Inspector," went on Dr. Bressingham, "that in the case of the deceased there were signs of three distinct sources of injury to the body—using the word injury in its exact meaning, of course."

"Three?" said Sloan, who could see that encouragement was still needed.

"Those inflicted—perhaps I should say acquired—during a game of Rugby on the Saturday afternoon previous to death." Dr. Bressingham didn't look a sporting type himself. He was pale and rather precisely dressed. "These injuries did not, of course, contribute to death but accounted for some of the contusions and abrasions on the body. There was a plaster dressing on one behind his left ear . . ."

"Play up! play up! and play the game!" murmured Sloan under his breath, making a note withal.

"There were also," continued the pathologist, "those injuries resulting from the deceased's car going off the road."

Sloan nodded. "We heard all about that."

"This was almost certainly as a consequence of his either having had diplopia . . ."

"Diplopia?" said Sloan. Crosby wouldn't be able to spell that.

"Double vision," translated the doctor.

"Ah."

"Either diplopia," repeated Dr. Bressingham, who was clearly not a man to make concessions to the demotic, "or of having gone to sleep at the wheel of his car from drug-induced drowsiness. Hyoscine relaxes smooth muscle."

Sloan did not know about smooth muscle and said so.

"Muscle not under voluntary control," said Dr. Bressingham. "That's why this particular drug is one of the main constituents of pre-medication." He waved a hand. "Given to patients before operations, that is . . ."

"Quite so," said Sloan somewhat shortly. He knew what pre-medication was. If there was one thing worse than being blinded by medical science it was being spoken to like a two-year-old.

"Too much leads to unconsciousness."

Sloan said that all the reports of the Calleshire County Constabulary Traffic Division on the inspection of Kenneth Carline's car confirmed the probability of this. "There were no exchange marks of any other vehicle having been in collision with the deceased's car. And no sign on the road surface of any involvement with one."

"No skid marks either," contributed Crosby, who took an interest in this melancholy aspect of fast driving.

"How serious were the road traffic accident injuries?" asked Sloan, automatically lapsing into police vernacular.

The pathologist gave a thin, humourless smile. "That, Inspector, depends entirely on which way you look at it."

Sloan pulled his head up sharply.

"The road traffic accident injuries weren't serious in themselves," said the doctor. "A fractured clavicle and some ankle lacerations . . ." he paused and then added significantly, "but . . ."

"But?" invited Sloan.

"But the consequences of those injuries were very serious indeed."

"How was that?" asked Sloan, allowing a slight edge to enter his voice. The games that people played were all very well but he had better things to do than engage in word ones with a strange pathologist.

"The House Surgeon in the Accident and Emergency Department," said Dr. Bressingham, "made the mistake of thinking that the deceased's drowsiness on admission was a consequence of concussion from a head injury sustained in the car accident."

"Very understandable," nodded Sloan.

"In the practice of medicine," said Dr. Bressingham loftily, "the excusable is not good enough."

"The art is long," Sloan heard himself saying aloud. Now that had come straight out of a memory of his own childhood. He'd had a mysterious rash on his hands when young and his mother had taken him to the surgery to ask the doctor what it was. And their general practitioner hadn't known and, being an honest man, had said so. By way of exculpation the doctor had added then, "The art is long . . ."

"And life is short. I know that." Dr. Bressingham completed the quotation brusquely. "But it's not good enough when human life is at stake."

Detective Inspector Sloan concluded without difficulty that young Dr. Bressingham was not likely to be the most popular of men with his colleagues. Perhaps hospital pathologists never were, having, as they always did, both plenty of time for their examinations as well as the last word.

"Of course," admitted the pathologist grudgingly, "the pupils of the eye are dilated in both cases."

"Which doesn't help," agreed Sloan. It sounded as if the house surgeon's lot—like the policeman's—was not a happy one.

"He did note on the admission record that the patient had an erythematous rash," said the doctor, "but did not appreciate its significance in poisoning by atropine, belladonna and hyoscine."

"I see," said Sloan, beginning to feel quite some sympathy for an unknown House Surgeon.

"In my opinion," said the pathologist, "arterial blood gases should be analysed in every case of deep coma."

"That would have helped, would it?" asked Sloan.

He should have known better. Nothing in medicine was as simple as that . . .

"It is impossible to say with any degree of certainty," said the pathologist in a hortatory manner, "whether the delay in first treating the patient for concussion and not poisoning was fatal or not."

Sloan nodded. It was the sort of theoretical positing in which the profession of law rejoiced and he was not naïve enough to believe that this interesting little legal point would have escaped Lucy Durmast's defence counsel . . . He pulled himself up with a jerk. Only Lucy Durmast didn't have a defence counsel, did she?

"However," continued Dr. Bressingham, "there is no doubt about the actual cause of death, which is what really matters."

"And that was hyoscine poisoning," said Sloan, tapping a wallet file. "I've got your report here, Doctor."

"What about the third set of injuries?" asked Detective Constable Crosby. "You said there were three."

The pathologist gave another thin smile. "Those," he said with precision, "that were a consequence of the injurious substance which the deceased had either taken or been given."

Sloan had forgotten that "injurious substance" was a medical euphemism for poison. "The Crown," he said, "will allege that it had been administered to the deceased by the accused in a meal of chili con carne."

"As vehicles for hyoscine go," responded the pathologist, "it is difficult to think of a better one."

Sloan raised an enquiring eyebrow.

Dr. Bressingham said, "A burning feeling in the mouth is another feature of hyoscine poisoning."

"Ah."

"And a dryness there."

Sloan nodded thoughtfully.

"And difficulty in swallowing."

Crosby sniffed. "Tailor-made."

"Nausea, too," said the pathologist.

"Can't stand it myself," remarked the constable. "Too hot."

"All symptoms that could follow a very powerful chili con carne," said Detective Inspector Sloan, sticking to the point.

"Agreed," said the pathologist. He paused and said carefully, "The presumption that the hyoscine was in the chili con carne is very strong."

"Presumption?" said Sloan.

"I can't confirm that it was," said Dr. Bressingham unexpectedly.

"You didn't find any of it in the stomach, then?"

"He lived too long after the meal for the stomach contents to be helpful in that respect."

"Where did you find it, then?" asked Sloan with a certain diffidence. Some of the nooks and crannies of the human body were terra incognita to a mere layman.

"The liver," said Dr. Bressingham. "Hyoscine is detoxified in the liver."

"And because Carline went into a coma there was none left in the stomach?"

"Because he continued to live after he had had the hyoscine, it had reached the liver by the time he died and I performed a post-mortem examination," said the doctor concisely.

"It's like Hunt the Thimble, isn't it?" remarked Crosby chattily.

Dr. Bressingham favoured him with a long hard stare. "Poisoning, Officer, is not something a pathologist ordinarily looks for after trauma."

"So," Sloan leapt speedily into speech, "there was a definite probability that, provided that the poisoned man actually got into his car and drove it away, that he would crash it?"

"Yes."

"And that—as happened when he was alive—his condition might be thought to be the result of that crash?"

"Yes."

"Unless you had examined the liver the poison would not have been found?"

"That is so."

"And what led you to do so?"

"There were certain macroscopic changes in its appearance."

"Daisy nearly pulls it off," observed Crosby insouciantly.

"Thank you, Doctor," said Sloan, rising to go. "You've been very helpful." Perhaps it wasn't too important after all that Lucy Durmast didn't have a defence counsel. It was beginning to look as though if she had engaged one, he'd have had to make bricks without straw.

For a brief moment the clinical technocrat on the other side of the desk mellowed into a man like other men. "Actually, Inspector, I don't mind telling you now . . ."

"Yes, Doctor?"

"It's my first murder case."

Detective Inspector Sloan, veteran policeman, nodded quite paternally. "I haven't forgotten making my first arrest, Doctor. I don't think you ever do." He picked up the wallet of papers from his desk. "Sorry to have taken up so much of your time."

He led the way out of the pathologist's office and into the corridor. They'd just check on Prince Aturu and the nuclear protest action group to be on the safe side and then report back to the Superintendent at Berebury.

Crosby jerked a thumb over his shoulder in the direction of the mortuary. "I bet his next job'll be a stiff one."

Melissa Wainwright, leader of the Action Against Marby Group, was dressed in blue denims and a tight blouse that looked as if it had been through the wash a hundred times or more, it was so faded. Her hair, on the other hand, did not appear to have been washed for some time. She lived, nevertheless, in relative comfort in one of the better parts of Calleford, which was where Detective Inspector Sloan and Detective Constable Crosby found her. She was positively eager to be interviewed by the police or anyone else —but, preferably, of course, the press.

She was, she explained shrilly to Sloan and Crosby, passionately against nuclear warfare on principle and the nuclear waste disposal plant at Marby juxta Mare in particular.

"Who knows what radiation leaks out?" she demanded rhetorically. "And they're not going to tell us, are they? Oh no! They'll cover up anything, they will." There was an unmistakable richness about her pronunciation of the word "they." "It's only when people start to die that anyone takes any notice. And then they'll say it's natural causes if they can."

Sloan cleared his throat preparatory to speaking.

"Or," she said before he could, "that the deaths aren't statistically significant."

He opened his mouth.

"You can keep your statistics," she said before he could speak, "and talk about people instead."

"Quite so." Sloan contrived to get a word in edgeways while Melissa Wainwright drew breath. He'd noticed before now how rarely statistics in support of an argument were ever countered by statistics demolishing it. If one side started playing the numbers game the other insisted on arguing in human terms.

"When politicians start talking about statistics," she said, "I always remind them about the statistician who was drowned in a river whose average depth was six inches. That shuts them up pretty quickly, I can tell you."

"I'm sure it does . . ." began Sloan, who had some figures in his own line of business at his fingertips. They were from an impeccable stable too—the Home Office—and they never convinced anyone of anything. People who were nervous about walking home through the streets alone in the dark never believed that statistically they were more likely to be murdered by a member of their own family than by anyone else. The goal of reaching the safety of their own homes had a hollow ring after that . . .

Perhaps the average woman might be prepared to believe that for her the bedroom was statistically the most dangerous place—he wouldn't know about that.

But it was.

And strangulation the most likely manner of her murder.

Men were at greatest risk in the kitchen. This had a great deal to do with the ready availability of knives. In every kitchen that Sloan had ever known, however much equipment of whatever degree of sophistication was there, there was always also one small sharp knife that was actually used for almost every task. It was always handy, too.

Sometimes it was even called a kitchen devil.

With babies it was the bathroom and drowning.

"But if there's one thing about statistics"—Melissa Wainwright was still in full flood—"that really gets my goat . . ."

"Yes, madam?" Detective Inspector Sloan would not have wanted to pontificate on Melissa Wainwright's marital status, but he was prepared to hazard the odd guess and calling her "madam" struck him as safest.

"It's when politicians start talking about the nuclear family that I really go berserk."

"Really?" said Sloan politely. He noticed that Detective Constable Crosby had taken Melissa Wainwright literally and was eyeing her in a distinctly speculative fashion. Young women in jeans and tight blouses were notoriously difficult to get hold of.

"The only nuclear family," she declaimed, "that people ought to be talking about is the one that isn't going to be here after the first attack. Instead of doing anything about that, they keep going on about their precious average of a father and a mother and two point two children." She sniffed. "And there's another thing they ought to be thinking about . . ."

"Yes?"

"That plant over at Marby is going to be dangerous for generations. How are future generations going to know that when we're all gone? Plain English won't mean anything after the balloon has gone up and there won't be any written records."

Sloan wasn't too worried about that. A legend of danger lasted longer than any signboard: it usually got built in to folk memory by a very primitive process indeed.

"So you see, Inspector . . ."

"We've come to see you about a different . . ." began Sloan, now that she'd had her own four-minute warning.

"What statistics do," she continued grumpily, "is confuse the issue."

"All politicians do that," said Sloan, forbearing to say anything about the tactics of certain defence counsel.

"And doctors," she added briefly. "Look at X rays. You try asking doctors exactly how dangerous they are . . ."

"What we want to ask you," Sloan interrupted her smoothly, "is if you knew a young man called Kenneth Carline."

Her face instantly assumed the mulish blankness of expression of the professional agitator intending to be deliberately unhelpful to the forces of law and order. "I wouldn't tell you if I did."

"Well-built, tallish, and worked for Durmast's, the civil engineers, on the Palshaw Tunnel," persisted Sloan.

A flicker of recognition crossed her face. "The man who was rushing about like a scalded cat at the opening after they saw our banner?"

"I daresay," said Sloan drily.

"I know who you mean," she said. "We called him the clean young Englishman."

As epitaphs go, Sloan himself wouldn't have asked for a better one. "You do remember him, then?"

A faint smile of reminiscence appeared on Melissa Wainwright's unadorned features. "He was the one who got sent up first to try to take the banner down. His boss sent him."

"I saw the picture," remarked Crosby from the sidelines. "It was in the local paper."

"But not the Minister," she said gleefully. "You didn't see a picture of the Minister opening the tunnel, did you?"

"No," said the constable.

"That's because he wouldn't be photographed under the banner and that"—she grimaced—"was where the ribbon was."

"And Kenneth Carline tried to get up to the banner?" asked Sloan. Almost all battles—even defeats—were remembered with advantages and it was Carline in whom they were interested now.

She nodded. "It was much too high, of course, and he couldn't do it." A reflective look came into her eyes. "That was before your mob arrived. One of them very nearly got up to it."

"Sergeant Watkinson," said Crosby.

"Then he fell," she said.

"Was pushed," countered Crosby.

"Broke his ankle, they said afterwards."

"Still limping," rejoined Crosby.

"Much too high to climb up from below."

"And sheer, the sergeant said," intoned Crosby. It was like the bidding and response of a religious ceremony.

"How did you get it up, then?" enquired Sloan.

"We didn't exactly put it up," she said.

"But . . ."

"We hung it down."

Sloan nodded. "That figures."

"We lowered it from above. About six of us."

"How did you get up there to do that?"

"Easy."

"There's a fence," said Sloan. "A high one."

"Fences have gates."

"Gates have locks," observed Sloan.

"We've got friends," she said.

"In high places, I suppose," said Crosby, "seeing that there's a hill there."

"Friends with keys," she said, stung.

"Who?" barked Sloan suddenly.

Her expression changed. It became mulish again. "I don't know."

"What do you mean by that, madam?" Sloan was at his most intimidating in an instant.

"I mean," she responded, "that the gate leading to the hill was unlocked."

"And you knew it would be?"

She stayed silent.

"I've read the report on the incident," said Sloan. "Whoever wrote it noted that your group had no ladders, hooks or any other equipment with you to enable you to climb over a very considerable fence erected to protect the access to the tunnel opening from above. From which, madam, we must therefore conclude that the

Action Group Against Marby proceeded to the tunnel entrance on the day of the official opening ceremony knowing that they could gain access."

"What if they did?"

"Someone must have arranged it."

"Well?"

"And given them the key."

"No."

"Told them that the gate would be unlocked, then."

"So?"

"Moreover," continued Sloan, "if that was the case whoever did leave the gate unlocked and apprised the Action Against Marby Group of the fact also left the key in the lock."

Melissa Wainwright did not speak.

"Officers," went on Sloan dispassionately, "who tried to gain access themselves by that route found the gate locked from the inside. That is why Sergeant Watkinson broke his ankle."

"There is such a thing as freedom of expression," exploded Melissa Wainwright, "even in a police state like this."

"There is also," said Sloan sternly, "such a thing as justice and it's every bit as important."

"What's that got to do with . . ."

"I need to know who your informant was."

"I don't know," she said.

"And I intend to find out."

"I don't know," she repeated.

"You were aware, though," insisted Sloan, "that the gate would be open." Every campaign manager was aware of the importance of holding the high ground.

She nodded without speaking.

"And that the key would be on the inside for you to use after you got in to help to keep the police out."

"Yes."

"How did you know that?"

"We had a tip-off." She bristled defensively. "You must know, Inspector, that there are plenty of people who would like to support us but daren't."

"It's a free country, madam."

"They've got their jobs to think of," she said.

"How did the tip-off reach you?" he persisted. Polemics were for politicians, not policemen. He'd learned that long ago. "It is important that we know."

She moistened her lips. "I had a telephone call."

"To you here at home?"

"Yes."

"Who rang you?"

"I tell you, Inspector, I don't know."

"A man or a woman?"

"A man."

"Who did he say he was?"

"He didn't."

"But . . ."

Her voice faltered for the first time. "He just called himself a friend at Durmast's and rang off."

NINE

Misturae—Mixtures

Lucy Durmast must have been one of the very few women in Her Majesty's Prison Cottingham Grange to whom an actual prison sentence had been a welcome pronouncement. For most of the women incarcerated there to exchange the state of being a prisoner on remand with all the privileges of an unconvicted—and therefore a potentially innocent—person with that of a convicted and sentenced inmate marked a very real decline in status.

There was a ranking order in prisons. They might not be a microcosm of the outside world in other ways—indeed they weren't —but this much they shared with the rest of society, and with most of the animal kingdom as well. Lucy had read George Orwell in her day and knew very well that though all animals were equal, some were more equal than others. Even so, it had come as something of a surprise to her to find how low those accused of killing somebody ranked in prison society.

And not because of the nature of the crime.

"Murder's usually only a family affair," one of her cellmates had sniffed.

"Mostly one-off breakers of the law, murderers," said another, an accomplished young "law-breaker" with a long record of convictions behind her.

"Not professional criminals," a prison officer had added in an unguarded moment.

Lucy had suppressed a smile. The jibe of amateur was the last thing she had expected in this environment. One way and another, Gentlemen v. Players somehow didn't seem to strike quite the right note. But she had noted the received wisdom of it all and kept her peace.

Murder charge or not, from the moment that Judge Eddington

had sentenced her to seven days' imprisonment for contempt of court her situation had changed. Literally. She had at once been moved across from the unconvicted wing of the prison to that of the convicted and lost the rights and privileges of the potentially not guilty. After that there was no possibility of having daily visitors descend upon her, of receiving and being able to send unlimited mail, and of choosing whether to have her meals brought in.

Since she had rigidly refused to see any visitors at all, had answered no mail and consistently declined her friend Cecelia Allsworthy's warm offer to bring home-baked delicacies from Braffle Episcopi to the gate of Cottingham Grange daily in a haybox, she felt less deprived than many others who had made the crossing of this great divide.

She had, however, read Cecelia's last letter with uncommon interest.

As usual it was cheerful as Cecelia could make it. ". . . Two different policemen came yesterday. I hadn't seen them before. It sounds as if they are going over the ground again so perhaps they'll find something helpful this time. There was a young constable—a bit gangling but trying hard. I rather liked him. The inspector didn't miss much—no one can say they aren't being really thorough . . . Hortense is still missing St. Amand-sur-Nesque. I'm afraid Braffle Episcopi does not stand up well in comparison with Provence! It's much colder and the flowers here in the spring do not compare with home, she tells me. I think I'll have to ask Ronald Bolsover if she can sit in his hot-house on her day off. At least his flowers should be up to scratch . . . Don't despair, will you, Lucy dear?"

In spite of this breath of fresh air from home, Lucy Durmast heard the clang of the cell door behind her with something approaching relief. The gates of the prison were locked against the outside world to keep it out as well as to the prisoner in. For the first time in her life she began to appreciate that the word "security" had two important but very different interpretations. From the outside looking in, it was one thing. From the inside looking out it was a horse of quite another colour.

There were two ways of looking out, too. She had discovered that very early on in herself and in other inmates as well: there had been something she remembered quite clearly which put it very well.

A prisoner looks out between bars
One sees mud, one sees stars . . .

Just at this moment though, Lucy Durmast wasn't looking out at
all. The warrant from the Court to the prison charged the governor with her care and safety as well as her security and as such it
was heartily endorsed in spirit by Lucy herself. Institutional life of
any sort did have drawbacks but it had advantages, too, and security was one of them. The shelter it provided could be most accept-
able in time of need . . .

Institutional life, though, was usually strong on rules and by her
determined silence she was breaking those rules.

The governor reminded her of this from time to time.

"The judge," she said to Lucy, "has indicated that he wishes to
be informed should you end your silence."

Justice, Lucy decided, was a game that needed the active partici-
pation of two players—the accuser and the accused. When one
party wouldn't play, then the game couldn't go on.

"Is that quite clear?" asked the governor crisply.

Not only, thought Lucy, couldn't the game go on without her
but she wasn't playing the game—which was something quite different. And probably more important, she thought, since Justice
seemed to be male. She started to consider this interesting point—
was it because of its Godlike stance, the blind female figure with
the Scales of Justice at the Old Bailey notwithstanding—when her
train of thought was interrupted.

"At any time," said the governor.

Lucy brought her mind back to the governor's office at Her
Majesty's Prison Cottingham Grange.

"It is usual when people are in prison for contempt of court,"
explained the governor, "for the judge to be informed should they
—er—have second thoughts on the matter."

If she did that, decided Lucy, she would at once be handed back
to the Court again for trial for murder. Then the Judge would
blow the whistle and the game would start in earnest. She shivered. There was something about the judge in the role of referee
that aroused uneasy memories of her school games field. The physical education teacher had been of the "jolly hockey-sticks" variety
(not to say vintage) and a stickler for the ethics of the world of

sport. One of her favourite edicts had been "The referee is right even when he or she is wrong."

Another frequent pronouncement had been on the importance of etiquette. At least, Lucy remembered wryly, she had acknowledged that ethics and etiquette were two different animals: she was never quite sure if the headmistress had. The etiquette of the games field, the teacher had insisted, required that the player should always behave afterwards as if the referee's judgement was correct.

Lucy could see that when the school team of St. Damien's played the first eleven of St. Cosmos's down the road it didn't matter very much; but carry the analogy into a court of law and it mattered a great deal. Especially if it were upon her—Lucy Mirabel Durmast —upon whom the judge was ruling. Suppose the judge *quae* referee were wrong?

And above criticism, too.

What about the ethic and the etiquette of the legal game?

"I might, perhaps, be able to put your mind at rest upon one point." The governor was conscientious to a degree. "Had you chosen to employ one, your legal adviser would, of course, have done so."

Lucy looked up but said nothing.

"Only if there is a verdict of guilty on the other charge . . ."

Even in prison, Lucy noted, everyone was mealy-mouthed about the mention of murder.

". . . will the jury be made aware of your sentence for contempt of court," continued the Governor. "It will then come under the category of previous convictions."

Lucy had forgotten all about the jury. Twelve good men and true came in somewhere, didn't they?

Had she forgotten them because she had only looked at the judge when she had been in Court or had it been more Freudian than that?

Twelve total strangers who came between her and her liberty. Twelve men and women plucked at random off a metaphorical Clapham omnibus to hold her destiny in their collective hands. All in the sacred name of that abstract conception called Justice— which meant something different to each person anyway. Twelve good citizens (and bad ones, too, very probably, seeing that they were all by definition human and no longer necessarily householders) swearing by Almighty God that they would faithfully try the several issues joined between Our Sovereign Lady the Queen and the Defendant . . .

There had been crimes that Queen Victoria hadn't been prepared to have on the Statute Book and said so. Lucy hadn't been very much interested in the history lesson at the time but she wished now she had paid more attention. She was suddenly curious to know which actions they were that Queen Victoria wouldn't join issue with . . .

The governor had clearly been pursuing quite a different train of thought. "The Court will be told about any previous convictions you have had only after a Guilty verdict has been given—if it has—and before sentence is passed."

The Law was as stately as quadrille. Lucy was irresistibly reminded of "The Lobster Quadrille" *Alice in Wonderland.* "Will you, won't you, will you, won't you, will you join the dance?"

Only nobody had asked her if she wanted to join the Law's dance. She was dancing by reason of *force majeur.* Literally, you might say. Whether she liked it or not. Or, more colloquially, seeing that it was all about the Law, without the option.

Lucy didn't hear what the governor said next because she was still thinking about the jury. Twelve good men and true—even though, when it came to the point, nobody actually knew how good they were, let alone true—had become arbiters a long time ago. Lucy knew that, too. She dimly remembered being taught that trial by ordeal had been the practice before trial by jury. Then the degree of effort the accused put into surviving the ordeal was the test. In those days everyone thought that those burdened by guilt would give up and that the innocent, buoyed up by just and righteous indignation and innocence—would struggle on. Too bad, for instance, if you just happened not to be able to swim.

She shivered. It didn't do to remember barbarity.

"You understand all this, I hope," said the governor.

What Lucy had just suddenly understood was where the common or garden phrase "sink or swim" had come from. She would never again use it lightly.

The governor was a persistent woman. "That jury won't be told anything about this sentence unless and until there is a guilty verdict."

It was what the jury would be told before the verdict that was troubling Lucy.

What the jury had to swear was that they would give true verdicts according to the evidence . . . Suppose the evidence wasn't true? Or simply not presented in Court? Did that mean that the jury would still be able to give a true verdict?

They didn't have to, of course. This dawned on Lucy rather belatedly. She realised a little late in the day that all the jury were charged with doing was reaching a true verdict according to the evidence—which was something much much simpler.

And very frightening indeed.

"Where to now, sir?" enquired Crosby as they left Melissa Wainwright's house in the outer suburbs of Calleford.

"The university," said Detective Inspector Sloan. "To see His Highness."

"Prince Aturu?"

"Successful criminal investigation is largely a matter of routine," said Sloan obliquely.

"Yes, sir," said the detective constable, who didn't mind where he was going as long as it was behind the steering wheel of a fast motor vehicle.

"Take me," instructed Sloan, "to Cremond College. That's the one the Prince is at."

Cremond College was one of the six colleges which comprised the University of Calleshire. It lay nearest to the Greatorex Library and was particularly popular with post-graduate students. Crosby brought the police car to a halt with something of a flourish at the entrance gate. Although Cremond College was one of the newer colleges of the Foundation it sported a Gothic-style arch. An engraved motto ran round the inside of the arch.

The detective constable picked out the words with difficulty. "*Auxilio . . . auxilio divino.*" He turned to Sloan. "What does that mean, sir?"

Sloan's schooling had been of the no-Latin-and-less-Greek variety. "Loosely translated," he grated, "it says 'Gawd help us.' Come along now, Crosby, let's not waste time." He led the way through the archway and cast a cynical eye over the quadrangle beyond. "If you ask me," he said gloomily, "the red-brick seems not so much Ivy League as in league with the ivy."

"It likes the mortar," said Crosby simply. "Sucks out the moisture in it. Like Count Dracula in . . ."

"I think we'd better talk to the dean first," said Sloan. All games involved keeping an eye on the ball but the detection one most of all. "Where's the porter's lodge?"

Dr. Adam Chelde, Dean of Cremond College, went out of his way to be helpful to the two policemen. "Of course I know Prince Aturu, Inspector. He's one of our post-graduate students. A very able young man, I understand. I think, though, that it would be fair to say that he is—er—something of a political theorist, too."

"A firebrand?" Sloan translated this without hesitation.

The dean coughed. "Most of the students who come to us from the—shall we say—the emergent nations are—er—usually activists by inclination."

"Not wanted at home," said Crosby.

"And if they happen to be economists as well . . ." the dean opened his hands expressively.

"A heady mixture," agreed Sloan.

"A difficult subject, economics," observed the dean in a detached way.

"They don't seem able to get it right, do they, sir?" remarked Sloan affably.

"It's a relatively new study, of course," said the dean. He was a distinguished palaeontologist.

Detective Inspector Sloan murmured something about Pharaoh's lean years. His mother was a great reader of the Bible.

"Ah," said Dr. Chelde instantly, "like a lot of people you are confusing good housekeeping with economic theory."

"Not the same thing?" enquired Sloan with irony.

"By no means."

"There were the foolish virgins, too, of course," said Sloan. He'd been made to go to Sunday School when young.

Detective Constable Crosby looked suddenly alert. Foolish virgins caused a lot of work down at the police station.

"The expression that I notice crops up most often in the Senior Common Room," said Dr. Chelde, "is corn in Egypt."

"What about 'Coals to Newcastle,'" said Crosby more parochially.

"But all that the economists will say is that their aim in life is to put a stop to feast and famine alike."

"Bully for them," murmured Crosby. "Did you know that if you put all the economists in the world end to end they still wouldn't reach a conclusion?"

"Dlasa," said Sloan firmly. "Where does the Kingdom of Dlasa fit into all this?"

The dean coughed again. "We do tend to find that most of our overseas students tend to relate all that they learn here in the first instance to their own home situations."

"Very understandable that, sir."

"Hopefully the—er—global view comes later."

"I understand," said Sloan, "that King Thabile is a hereditary monarch."

"The situation," said the dean, "where you have infant sciences married to newly developing nations does tend to make for difficulties." Whenever the press asked for a statement from the University of Calleshire, Dr. Adam Chelde was always the one who was put up to make it. His pontifications were so general that it was practically impossible to isolate the particular.

"And," said Sloan, policeman not pressman, "that the King has embarked on building a new capital city in Dlasa."

"So I understand," responded the dean. "The Prince has been—er—most eloquent on the subject." He paused and added, "Not to say outspoken."

Sloan cocked his head alertly. "He has, has he?"

"In spite of the fact that his tutor has constantly reminded him of the natural tendency of all men to strive to be remembered in—er—stone or some comparable long-lasting material . . ."

Sloan nodded. His mother would have reminded him of what had been said on the subject in Ecclesiastes: some there be who have no memorial.

The dean waved a hand. "The Pyramids, Stonehenge, this college . . ." Dr. Chelde achieved this step from the general to the particular with greater ease.

"But the Prince was unconvinced?" suggested Sloan.

"Totally," said the dean. "However I understand he buckled down to work on his thesis all right in the end."

"It wasn't on bride-prices by any chance, was it?" enquired Crosby, who was unmarried. The idea had tickled his fancy.

Dr. Chelde shook his head. "I am told that in the first instance there had been some discussion about its being on the relationship between the smaller Dlasian and English weights and measures."

"Feet and inches?" said Sloan, who wasn't and never would be a thinker in metric.

"Barleycorns," said the Dean. "There are three to the inch here."

"I didn't know that," said Sloan gravely.

"And the apothecary's grain. That has an agricultural base, too."

"Rod, pole and perch," said Crosby suddenly.

"In Dlasa," said the dean, "I believe that the spear is the linear unit." He brightened. "In Russia it used to be the vershok."

"Really?" said Sloan politely. He wasn't sure if he needed to know that.

"And the vershok is the exact diameter of an American golf ball," said the academic. "One point six eight inches."

"But that wasn't what the Prince's thesis was about after all?" hazarded Sloan.

Dr. Chelde shook his head. "It was on something—er—rather less cognate, I fear."

Sloan looked up enquiringly.

"And perhaps in the end less useful," said Dr. Chelde.

Sloan asked what the Prince's thesis had actually been about.

"The political usury of foreign aid," said the Dean sadly. "I don't know if he finished it."

"We can ask him," said Sloan, starting to move forward.

"I'm afraid that that will be a little difficult, Inspector."

Sloan stopped. "How so?"

"Prince Aturu's not here any more." The dean looked at the two policemen. "Didn't you know?"

"No," said Sloan.

"He had to go back to Dlasa at the beginning of February."

"Had to?" echoed Sloan.

"Very suddenly," said the Dean.

"Why?"

"He was recalled. His allowance was stopped by King Thabile."

"For what reason?" asked Sloan.

"Kings don't give reasons."

"You must have had some idea . . ."

"All fathers see their sons as rivals," said Dr. Chelde.

"Psychology is nothing to be afraid of," remarked Crosby.

"Oedipus," said the Dean, adding rather neatly after a pause, "Rex. Dear me, yes," he gave a positively old-fashioned chortle, "Oedipus Rex. I must remember that."

"Prince Aturu of Dlasa," said Sloan gamely.

"Absolute monarchs tend to dislike controversy politics," said the dean. "That's another thing entirely."

"I can understand that," said Sloan. He didn't like them himself. It was when people got hurt.

"Whatever the reason, Inspector, I can assure you that Prince Aturu was on his way back to Dlasa within the day."

"And nothing's been heard from him since?"

"Nothing at all."

TEN

Vitrellae—Glass capsules

"Dr. Livingstone, I presume," said Superintendent Leeyes grandly. "That's who you think you are, I suppose, Sloan?"

"No, sir."

"And then"—the superintendent glared across his desk—"I expect we'd have to send Crosby out into the jungle afterwards to look for you."

"Not at all, sir."

"Like that other fellow—I forget his name."

"H. M. Stanley, sir."

"On second thoughts," said Leeyes, "perhaps not Crosby. He'd be bound to tread on a crocodile or something."

"It wasn't that sort of search that I had in mind," said Sloan.

"He might even start a tribal war. If he upsets them like he upsets me . . ."

"Just a simple enquiry to Dlasa, sir, that's all."

"If it's all so simple," snapped Leeyes, "what's the problem?"

"They don't have a police force to ask."

"What?" said Leeyes. "No men in blue?"

"None, sir." He hesitated. "They don't have any law, you see."

Leeyes grunted. "No point in having the one without the other, I suppose."

"Not really, sir." Now he came to think of it, Sloan could only agree.

The superintendent looked up keenly. "Does that mean, Sloan, that they don't have any lawyers in Dlasa either?"

"It does. The Dean of Cremond College explained to me that that was why Prince Aturu had read Economics even though he'd got a lawyer's mind . . ."

Superintendent Leeyes's expression was quite inscrutable.

"And a politician's ambition," added Sloan.

"A nasty combination." The superintendent shook his head.

Sloan nodded. It was easily as effective a recipe for difficulty as economics married to activism.

"Can't you talk to their high commissioner in London?" asked Leeyes briskly.

"They haven't got one, sir," answered Sloan. "I had wondered about the Foreign and Commonwealth Office . . ."

"White man's burden and white man's grave," pronounced Leeyes sourly.

"Pardon, sir?"

"The Foreign and Commonwealth Office," said Leeyes. "Between the two they cover the lot."

"Er—quite so, sir." Sloan took a deep breath. "I propose to get in touch with them."

"They'll be about as much good as the old Home and Colonial grocery store," forecast Leeyes, "but there's no harm in trying, I suppose." He hitched his shoulders. "This Kingdom of Dlasa, Sloan, is it a friendly nation or was it a former British Protectorate?"

"Neither, sir," said Sloan carefully. He'd done his homework as well as he could. "It appears to be what is known as non-aligned."

"I see," said Leeyes. "*Rouge et noir.*"

"No, sir, not exactly. Not Red . . . just non-aligned."

"What I mean," said Leeyes with dignity, "was that the King was playing both sides of the roulette table. *Rouge et noir.* Not *noir* and therefore *rouge.*"

"Sorry, sir. I understand." The only sort of roulette that Sloan knew anything about was the Russian variety much favoured by those who could not even make up their own minds about suicide.

"Hedging their bets," sniffed Leeyes, abandoning Franglais. "Can't say I blame them."

"No, sir."

The superintendent lifted his head. "I take it, Sloan, that Dlasa is what it is fashionable these days to call underdeveloped?"

"Yes, sir," replied Sloan. There were international standards that measured this. With or without laws and a police force Dlasa was underdeveloped.

"And are you trying to tell me, Sloan, that there's a connection between Kenneth Carline's death and Prince Aturu's being called back to Africa so suddenly?"

"It may only be a coincidence, sir." Detective Inspector Sloan's reply was studied. The Superintendent did not allow coincidence in detection.

"Well?" Leeyes did not rise.

"The only people," swept on Sloan, "who would seem able to tell for certain are either dead, dumb or departed."

"There's that deputy chairman fellow . . ."

"Ronald Bolsover," agreed Sloan. "I'm going to see him again. Not that he mentioned anything about any Dlasians being in Calleshire when I saw him before."

"What about the accused?" asked Leeyes. "Did she know this Prince Aturu?"

"She's not saying, sir, is she?"

"Can't we find out?"

"Her friend at Braffle Episcopi might know," said Sloan. "Mrs. Cecelia Allsworthy. She's very helpful."

"In our work," declared Leeyes didactically, "you learn that you always have to ask yourself why someone is being helpful."

"Of course, sir. Naturally." Sloan hadn't been born yesterday—which was one reason why he didn't say so. The other was that he had his pension to think of. "But even—er—suspect information is better than no information at all." He paused and thought. Did he really mean that? "There is another point, sir. Even if there is a link between Prince Aturu and the murdered man neither Ronald Bolsover nor Cecelia Allsworthy might have known about it."

"Or they might have done," countered Leeyes promptly, "and not told us."

"True, sir."

"All we really know for certain," pronounced the superintendent, "was that Kenneth Carline died from an overdose of hyoscine and that Lucy Durmast is speaking to neither man nor beast. Right?"

"Right," said Sloan.

"And now we also know that Prince Aturu left Cremond College at the University of Calleshire in a great hurry the week after Kenneth Carline died? Right?"

"Right."

"Doesn't amount to much, Sloan, does it?" he sniffed.

"Oh, there's one more thing, sir." Sloan told the superintendent about the telephone call Melissa Wainwright had said she had had before the anti-nuclear demonstration.

"How did she know that the message had come from Durmast's?" challenged Leeyes with speed.

"She didn't," said Sloan, "except that presumably only somebody at Durmast's would have had access to a key to the gate in the protective fencing."

"Was Prince Aturu a nuclear campaigner seeing as he was up at the university?" A philosopher wouldn't have liked the superintendent's leap in logic—it smacked of the classic "When did you stop beating your wife?" but Sloan knew better than to argue.

"The dean," he replied neutrally, "was going to make some enquiries about that for us, sir."

Leeyes drummed his fingers on the table. "Are you suggesting, Sloan, that it was Kenneth Carline who let these protesters on to the tunnel site to disrupt the opening ceremony?"

"I'm only saying, sir, that the person who actually did so told Melissa Wainwright that he was from Durmast's, which was a funny thing to do in the circumstances."

Leeyes grunted. "The deceased had some leaflets about the nuclear waste disposal plant at Marby juxta Mare in his car when it was found, didn't he? You haven't forgotten that, had you, Sloan?"

"No, sir."

Leeyes looked thoughtful. "Does it follow that a young man capable for whatever reason of helping to ruin the official opening ceremony of a tunnel built by the firm for which he works is also capable of attempting to sabotage that same firm's next contract to build a capital city in Africa?"

"I don't know, sir."

"In alliance with another young man who does not appear to know on which side his bread is buttered."

"Kenneth Carline's friends," ventured Sloan, "told me that the Prince thought he was saving his country."

"I have a fair grasp of the politics of this country," said Leeyes heavily, "to say nothing of those of the Calleshire County Council, but those of Africa are beyond me."

"Yes, sir."

"I do know, though," mused Leeyes with apparent irrelevance, "that Dlasa is the sort of place where they used to have missionaries for dinner."

"Did they, sir?"

"Moreover, they may not even now know that eating people is wrong."

"No, sir."

"I wonder exactly what's happened to Prince Aturu," the superintendent mused.

Sloan was suddenly uneasy. "I must say I hadn't thought about that, sir."

Leeyes waved an admonitory hand. "You should, Sloan, you should. Not that there's a lot we can do about it."

"No, sir," If anything, Sloan's uneasiness deepened. As a rule the superintendent's responses to almost all overseas situations were of the despatching of a gunboat nature. So far he hadn't mentioned action at all . . .

"Let us hope," said Leeyes enigmatically, "that the only croaking Prince Aturu of Dlasa has done is as a frog."

Detective Inspector Sloan could think of absolutely nothing to say.

"Lucy interested in nuclear warfare, Inspector?" Cecelia Allsworthy shook her head vigorously. "No, not as far as I know."

"I see, madam." The two policemen had patently interrupted Cecelia at her pottery wheel. It was not Mrs. John Allsworthy, wife of the Squire of Braffle Episcopi, who had welcomed them to the Manor House but Cecelia Allsworthy, sometime art student at the Slade, quondam artist and now asking no higher designation than that of simple potter. She had come through to see them a little flustered, her hands still bearing traces of clay, her face smudged.

"And I'm sure I would have known, Inspector." She detached her mind with difficulty from considering the angle of the neck of the vase she was working on. She had been thinking how it was that the differences between the cultures of India and China could be somehow epitomised in the rake of a vase's neck and the concept had suddenly started to fascinate her. Where other people talked about national characteristics she had begun to think in terms of a curve. Did it go for Samian and Etruscan ware, too, she had been wondering when the front doorbell had rung. A vision of the Portland vase drifted into her mind and out again as she turned to her *au pair* girl. "Hortense, be an angel and go and put the kettle on for a pot of tea for these gentlemen."

"*Mais oui*, Cecelia . . ."

Where other people talked about national characteristics she thought about vases. She supposed that Anglo-Saxon overlaid with Norman—rather like the parish church of Braffle Episcopi—influenced by everything she'd ever read and seen and been taught made the compound style that she was producing now, but she wasn't quite satisfied. What she was seeking was something even more cognate . . .

"Come along in, Inspector, and sit down." She took one of the twins out of the young French girl's arms as she went towards the door and then, a moment later, took a few steps after her and called out "I'll infuse the tea myself, Hortense. Just see to everything else."

"*Certainement* . . ."

"She's very good," said Cecelia Allsworthy, coming back, "but she can't make tea properly. The French never can, you know."

"Yes, madam," said Sloan. Had Superintendent Leeyes been with Sloan and Crosby at the Manor House at Braffle Episcopi he would undoubtedly have agreed with Mrs. Allsworthy. Their superior officer's view on what the French were incapable of doing well had merely been exacerbated—not changed—by war and had much in common with those of the late Duke of Wellington.

Cecelia frowned. "I daresay Lucy didn't like the idea of a nuclear winter any more than anyone else does but that isn't the point, is it?"

"No, madam."

"But from the way some people carry on you might think it is."

"Some people get very worked up," observed the policeman mildly.

"A great mistake," said Mrs. Allsworthy at once. "I can think of a lot worse fates than dying at the same time as everyone I love. Save a lot of pain and grief."

Sloan bowed his head to a higher realism than he had thought of. It was a view of atomic bombing that he hadn't encountered before: that didn't feature in any argument. "Is that what Lucy Durmast thought too?"

She wrinkled her face in an attempt at recollection. "All I know is that she agreed with me that the actual plant at Marby juxta Mare was impressive to look at—which it is—but she didn't wear a badge or anything like that." Suddenly Cecelia Allsworthy's face lit up. "I do remember something though, Inspector."

"Yes?"

"It was the day when we went over to Marby to see how the plant was getting on. It's really quite stylish, you know. They haven't skimped on the design side—one of the building is a perfect rhomboid."

"And?"

"It sounds a bit silly really when it's repeated in cold blood."

"Go on." Cold blood had come into somebody's calculations already anyway.

"Well, there was one of those posters stuck on a wall there about giving up nuclear arms and advertising a protest march."

"They were all over the place," agreed Sloan.

"Lucy said that it was legs they should give up as well."

"That's what I wanted to know, madam," Sloan cleared his throat. It told him in a sentence that Lucy Durmast was no antinuclear zealot. "You wouldn't happen to know if the deceased—Kenneth Carline, I mean—held strong views on unilateral disarmament, would you?"

Cecelia Allsworthy shook her head again as she settled one of her young sons beside his brother in a play-pen. "No, although I can't honestly say that I really knew what Kenneth's own opinion was about anything. He didn't go around saying what he thought about things anyway." She gave a quick shrug. "You don't, do you, in your first job? It's too important, isn't it, to begin with, for free speech."

That aspect of employment hadn't occurred to Sloan. It was different in the police force anyway. You weren't there to have views. Just to uphold the right of everyone else to express theirs, which was different.

"Besides," continued Mrs. Allsworthy, "Kenneth Carline didn't join the firm until after the tunnel was well under way. He took over from a man who was killed in a road accident in Yorkshire."

"Did he?" said Sloan. Durmast's had been unlucky in their design engineers. To lose one parent, so to speak, might be regarded as a misfortune; to lose both looks like carelessness.

"Anyway," swept on Cecelia Allsworthy realistically, "Lucy

knew far too well how much the Palshaw Tunnel meant to her father and to Durmast's for her to start getting caught up with the Marby nuclear protesters. And so, I should have thought, did Kenneth Carline."

"I can see that it meant a good deal," murmured Sloan. What he couldn't for the life of him see was what any of it had to do with one very junior civil engineer dying after a meal with the boss's daughter.

"I'll never forget the party they had when the pilot tunnels met halfway," said Cecelia Allsworthy, picking off a stray piece of ball clay from her arm. "It was just after I married and came here and everyone was so excited. Do you know that when the two ends of the tunnel met in the middle they were only a few inches out?"

"Really?" Civil engineering was a closed book to the policeman but that opposite ends of tunnels and bridges should meet as planned was something that Sloan had always found impressive too.

"It is particularly important," said Lucy Durmast's friend, "when it's a sub-aqueous excavation."

"I can see that," said Sloan gravely.

"Water, water everywhere and not a drop to drink," remarked Crosby insouciantly. "If they don't meet, that is."

"Lucy said it was the equivalent of topping out in the building trade," went on Cecelia, "and that there should be a celebration. They were ahead of schedule, too—Ronald Bolsover was still at his place in Provence when it happened. He wasn't even due back for another week, which shows how far on they were. They actually finished on time, too."

That, thought Sloan, was pretty nearly as impressive these days as meeting in the middle without mishap. "Everyone must have been very pleased," he murmured, wondering what it all had to do with the job in hand. His job, that is, as head of Berebury's Criminal Investigation Department.

"Anyway, as soon as the Edsway end had met the Palshaw end, Lucy's father started going off to Africa." Cecelia Allsworthy leant over the play-pen and separated two little boys who might have been physical twins but who certainly weren't spiritual ones. "Bill said his part in the tunnel was as good as done and he could safely leave the rest to everyone else—and to the tunnel-boring machine, of course."

Detective Inspector Sloan nodded his comprehension.

"Except"—she gave another of her quick smiles—"that Bill always called it the boring tunnel machine."

Sloan knew other people like Bill Durmast who flourished only on challenge and constant change, and who fled routine as the Devil incarnate.

"He was off to Africa as soon as you could say 'knife' after that," said Cecelia.

That brought Sloan to something else. He asked her if she knew Prince Aturu of Dlasa.

"No, Inspector." She shook her head. "None of the people to do with the Mgongwala contract have been to England at all. Lucy told me that. That's why her father had to be away so much."

Sloan explained that Prince Aturu had been in England as a post-graduate student but that he had suddenly left the University of Calleshire without anyone knowing why.

"Perhaps he was homesick," she suggested. "Hortense is suffering dreadfully from homesickness. She's simply living for the day when she can get back to St. Amand-sur-Nesque."

"Prince Aturu was violently opposed to the building of Mgongwala," Sloan informed her. To his mind and from what he had heard, the Prince was more likely to have been sick of home rather than the other way round.

"Perhaps the climate had something to do with it," said Mrs. Allsworthy. "Poor Hortense just can't get used to Calleshire in the spring after being brought up in the South of France." She grinned. "I've even asked Ronald Bolsover if she could go over and sit in his hot-house on her day off. Not like Bill Durmast. He loves the heat of Africa."

"He was there though, wasn't he, for the official opening?" asked Sloan.

"Oh yes." She nodded and added solemnly, "Lucy and I decided that that was a rite of passage."

"Very good," acknowledged Sloan. All policemen had some sociology thrust down their throats these days, whether they liked it or not.

"And Lucy and I went up to London to choose her outfit." Cecelia Allsworthy, who had a casual elegance all her own, said earnestly, "The Lord Lieutenant's wife always dresses so well and the

Minister's wife was coming too, you see. Lucy didn't want to let her father down."

"You've got to keep your end up at an opening ceremony," agreed Sloan. Keeping the flag flying in Court and in Her Majesty's Prison Cottingham Grange wouldn't be quite so easy but all the evidence pointed to Lucy Durmast doing her best then and now.

"Mrs. Othen—she's the County Surveyor's wife—was in mink," recounted Cecelia Allsworthy. "That upset some of the nuclear protesters too. Lucy told me she heard one of them shout 'Fur coats are beautiful on animals but ugly on people.'"

"Rites of passage are always a strain," said Sloan solemnly. The sociologists had taught that, too. The fur lobby was something else . . .

"This one certainly was from all that I heard about it," said Cecelia. "Mrs. Clopton—Clopton's were the contractors—had gone overboard a bit in pink."

"Not an easy colour," agreed Sloan. His wife, Margaret, had long ago averred that no woman over thirty could ever look really smart in pink.

"Especially in winter," put in Detective Constable Crosby unexpectedly. "A cold day, wasn't it?"

"Very."

"Sergeant Watkinson said it was cold enough to do some serious damage to a brass monkey," said Crosby, "and that was before he broke his leg."

"In the end," said Mrs. Allsworthy regretfully, "it didn't matter all that much what anyone wore. All that anyone looked at was that great big banner."

"I hear it came right down over the top of the tunnel entrance," said Sloan.

"Portal," said Cecelia. "You're not supposed to call it an entrance. Ah, here's Hortense . . . Is the kettle really boiling?"

The French girl said, "Really boiling, Cecelia, I promise," and set down a tray with everything on it for tea save the teapot.

While Mrs. Allsworthy went off in the direction of the kitchen and the really boiling kettle, Detective Inspector Sloan took his first good look at Hortense. She was wearing a mottled green skirt and a burgundy-coloured blouse, and she was younger than he had thought at first. "And how do you like England, mademoiselle?" he asked kindly.

Detective Constable Crosby took his first good look at Hortense too—and then another.

Hortense answered Sloan but she looked at Crosby. "It is very cold in the spring," she enunciated as carefully as Eliza Doolittle. "At home now it is warm and very beautiful."

Crosby straightened his collar.

"I miss the . . . the smells so much." She looked up anxiously. "Is that the wrong word?"

"Scents, miss," said the detective constable huskily. "That's the word you're looking for."

"Perfume," said Hortense. "That is the word I seek. I come from Provence, *messieurs,* you see. From a jasmine farm."

All the perfumes of Arabia, thought Sloan inconsequentially. That was something that had cropped up in a famous murder.

"I miss the mimosa, too," she said to Crosby, lowering her eyes just a trifle.

The detective constable looked at the petite French girl as if she were made of porcelain and might break at any moment.

"Especially in spring." She lowered her voice a fraction too.

"The spring . . ." agreed Crosby in a strangled voice.

"Tea!" announced Mrs. Cecelia Allsworthy, coming back into the room with a teapot of a thoroughly satisfactory size.

ELEVEN

Vapores—Inhalations

Ronald Bolsover's secretary said, "He won't keep you waiting long, Inspector. He's got someone with him at the moment."

Sloan could see this for himself. The firm of William Durmast, Ltd., was situated in a house with a very attractive Georgian front in the middle of the Rushmarket in Calleford. The back of the building was another matter. It was a higgledy-piggledy of periods and styles, and wherever possible, walls and sections of roof had been cut away and large windows inserted. In a design office natural light was at a premium and Sloan was aware that Ronald Bolsover needed it for his work as much as anyone. There were three architect's drawing stands in his room and two interior walls had been removed to hip height and glass substituted to borrow as much light as possible from the outside world.

As Inspector Porritt had faithfully reported, Ronald Bolsover's secretary would have been in a position to see her employer's every action but not hear what was being said in his room. Sloan stood by the deputy chairman's secretary's desk now and watched Bolsover through the glass partition as he was talking to another man.

The secretary misinterpreted his interest for impatience. "Mr. Bolsover's nearly finished with his other visitor."

"Thank you, miss. There's no hurry at all." He tapped his papers. "We're just checking up on the day Kenneth Carline died."

"Poor Ken," she said at once, adding defiantly, "and poor Lucy even if she did do it."

"You knew them both?" He should have remembered that.

"Of course," she said. "Ken had been working here for the best part of two years and I remember Lucy as a little girl."

"Aaaarh," said Sloan as encouragingly as a doctor. "You won't have forgotten that Monday morning, then."

"Certainly not. He—Ken, that is—had arranged to see Mr. Bolsover at half-past eleven. Mr. Bolsover had told me so himself the previous Friday afternoon, and I put it in his diary. He was very busy that day what with Mr. Durmast being in Africa and having this appointment at Palshaw at two o'clock about the tunnel, to say nothing of its being a Monday, which is always a rush."

"Quite so," said Sloan. Work came in unexpected bursts down at the police station too, but not as a rule on Monday mornings. Crime tended to build up towards the end of the day and towards the end of the week. The crescendo usually came on Saturday evenings.

"And Ken came down from his own room upstairs just before the half hour." She looked rueful. "I must say he looked a real sight what with his bruises and everything. He said 'You should have seen the other fellow, though, Mary.' I said Rugby wasn't a very nice game if that's what happened to people playing it, but he only laughed. I could tell Mr. Bolsover didn't like to see him looking like that, though, because after Ken had gone in there I saw him open up his first-aid box and put a piece of sticking plaster on a graze behind Ken's ear that was still oozing."

"Mr. Bolsover didn't give him anything to eat or drink though, did he?" murmured Sloan, one eye still on the deputy chairman of Durmast's. Ronald Bolsover was still talking animatedly to his visitor, using his hands in a Gallic way a good deal as he spoke.

"No, Inspector." She was adamant about that. "There's a coffee machine in the front hall anyway. Everyone uses that when they want a drink."

"How long was Kenneth Carline in with Mr. Bolsover?" asked Sloan, although he knew the answer already.

The secretary repeated what she had told Inspector Porritt. "About half an hour. They were looking at the Palshaw Tunnel plans for most of the time. Then Ken came out and asked if he could use my telephone to ring Lucy Durmast."

"You actually heard him talking to her, then?" said Sloan. Mr. Bolsover's visitor was beginning to show signs of preparing to take his departure.

The secretary nodded. "Ken asked Lucy if he could call at the Old Rectory to collect some plans from her father's study before he met Mr. Bolsover at the tunnel at Palshaw. Then she must have asked him to stay to lunch because he said 'Thank you, that would be very nice' and that he would try to be there by one o'clock." She looked Sloan straight in the eye. "He was like that. Always polite."

"I'm sure," murmured Sloan.

"Lucy must have asked Mr. Bolsover to lunch too because I heard Ken say he was sure he wouldn't be able to come as well because he'd got something else to do before they met at Palshaw at two o'clock."

Sloan listened attentively. What the secretary was saying gibed in every way with what Cecelia Allsworthy had told him about Lucy Durmast's end of the conversation. The spur-of-the-moment invitation and the preparation of the scratch meal appeared to be genuine. There was, of course, nothing to prevent them both being the ingredients of a murder . . .

"And what was it Mr. Bolsover had to do," asked Sloan, "and so couldn't go to lunch with Miss Durmast as well?"

The secretary pointed to her notebook. "His letters. Mr. Bolsover doesn't like using a Dictaphone. He likes his letters taken down properly in shorthand."

Sloan could see that he was expected to see the traditional as a sign of virtue and accordingly nodded his approval.

"Mr. Bolsover dictated a lot of work to me right up to lunch-time. In fact," she said, "rather after lunch-time. I was very late going to lunch myself that day and Mr. Bolsover couldn't have had time for anything much to eat himself. Not if he was going to get to Palshaw by two o'clock, which was when his appointment was for."

"I see," said Sloan. Mr. Bolsover's present visitor had at last risen to his feet and had begun to take his farewells. It was rather curious, seeing him do it without being able to hear a word through the glass, not unlike watching an old-fashioned mime.

Or a silent film, perhaps.

Actions without words.

The death of Kenneth Carline had been curiously without speech, too.

Almost a dumb show.

A sudden unexpected invitation followed by a slow and unexpected death.

And even after that wordlessness.

Except for a disembodied voice talking about gates that would be open that should have been locked and keys that should not have been there at all. Which might or might not have had anything to do with the situation.

There were absences which were disturbing, too, rather than presences, which might have been helpful.

The accused's father had gone abroad before the action began: Prince Aturu so soon afterwards as to represent a further worry. Where did the African Kingdom of Dlasa and its new town at Mgongwala come into all this?

If it did.

Sloan wasn't even sure if it would help if he saw a replay of such action as had taken place here at Durmast's. The mental imagery of the rewinding of a silent film though made him turn his mind to Crosby. He shifted his gaze to see whether the detective constable had been as absorbed by the peepshow the other side of the glass screen as he had been. Crosby, it was apparent, wasn't even looking in Ronald Bolsover's direction. He had drifted over towards one of the windows and was staring out over the assorted roofscapes towards the Minster.

A movement inside the goldfish bowl that was Bolsover's office attracted Sloan's attention. The deputy chairman's visitor was making for the door. Sloan was struck by how unselfconscious both men appeared behind their screens: the play within the play, almost. A similar sense of isolation must be engendered in patients in hospital being barrier-nursed: often enough they had to be content with a glimpse of their loved ones through glass. A distant wave wasn't the same as warm human contact . . .

"Mr. Bolsover will see you now, Inspector," murmured the secretary at Sloan's side.

"Come along, Crosby," commanded Sloan.

The constable turned reluctantly from the window. "Did you know, sir, that on a clear day you can see . . ."

"Crosby!"

Ronald Bolsover rose to his feet as they entered. "I'm sorry to have kept you waiting, gentlemen . . ."

In Her Majesty's Prison Establishment for Women and Girls at Cottingham Grange there was also a certain amount of standing upon ceremony before a visitor was shown into the presence of the person holding the reins of office. Rather more in fact than obtained at the headquarters of the firm of William Durmast. At

Cottingham Grange it was the governor's room outside which other people waited. And in Lucy Durmast's case she was one of a considerable queue.

First there were those who wanted to see the governor and after them there were those whom the governor wanted to see. Lucy came into the latter class. She didn't know why. She had simply been told that morning by her wing officer that the governor wished to see her. Even had she not been adopting her Trappist-like stance and had chosen to ask what the governor wanted to see her about she was doubtful if she would have been given an answer. The normal give-and-take of human exchange was conspicuous by its absence in the highly structured world of prison.

One by one those in front of Lucy were admitted to the governor's office and their problems and transgressions dealt with. Lucy was no longer sure that the two were not indistinguishable—that was something that a prison sentence had taught her. More than once what she had learned while listening to her fellow prisoners talking had sent her mind back to one of her set books in the sixth form at school. Once read she had put it behind her and turned to more interesting works of literature. In her wildest dreams she had never expected to be giving fresh thought to Samuel Butler's *Erewhon*.

The first thing that all the class remembered was that "Erewhon" was an anagram of "Nowhere" and that was certainly true of the land that Samuel Butler described. The second thing that nobody forgot was that in "Erewhon" it was illness and disease that incurred moral obliquity, and crime that became a matter for condolence and treatment. Butler would have put the sick in prison and the committers of crime in hospital. When young and still sure of finding an answer to life's perplexities this had seemed arcane treatment indeed.

The queue outside the governor's office shuffled forward, but Lucy was almost unaware of being in it.

She was less starry-eyed now and more inclined to the view that there weren't as many solutions as there were problems. Her own shining lance of youth had been both tarnished and blunted by Kenneth Carline's death and what had followed. Her mind slid away from both Samuel Butler and Kenneth Durmast as she thought about Don Quixote and his lance. She felt a momentary flash of fellow feeling with that eccentric knight. Tilting at wind-mills was easier and safer than tilting at a lot of other things.

"Quiet there!" someone shouted.

Lucy didn't even hear them. She was considering Samuel Butler's answer. It had taken on a new interest since she had been in prison herself. There were those about her in plenty in Cotting-ham Grange who, even to Lucy's lazy eye, were suitable cases for treatment. Her doctor grandfather had always linked illness with guilt—or had it been guilt with interest? She wasn't sure now which it had been and was pursuing this interesting train of thought when someone called her name. She looked up.

"Give your name and number to the governor," said a com-manding voice.

Lucy stood in front of the governor silent but in an attitude of polite attention. Dumb insolence would have been alien to both her nature and her intention.

"Ah, Durmast," said the governor pleasantly. "We have a little problem about something in your post."

Lucy looked up. Incoming mail had not been one of the things that had worried her in Cottingham Grange. Her father was no great correspondent at the best of times: when totally immersed in a project he seldom put pen to paper other than on a drawing board, although he might have written home for something he had forgotten. Letters from Cecelia Allsworthy couldn't conceivably pose a problem . . .

"It's not a letter exactly," said the governor. There was some-thing in a folder on her desk but Lucy couldn't see what. "More of a—well, a communication really."

Lucy looked quite blank.

"We wondered if you could perhaps explain it to us before it is given to you." She coughed. "You will understand that we have always to be very careful in the—er—custodial situation."

Lucy had heard a variety of euphemisms for prison—mostly from fellow inmates and quite unrepeatable—but "custodial situa-tion" was a new one to her.

"It would appear," continued the governor, "to have a symbolic meaning of some sort."

Lucy tilted her head sharply.

"The message—if indeed it contains a message—is conveyed on a sort of raffia." The governor opened the file on her desk and produced a rough square of loosely woven dried grass matting. "As you will see there is a drawing of a highly ritualised nature of a bird in the top left-hand corner, and in the bottom right what appears to be a sword of some sort."

Lucy paled.

"Some hair," the governor continued her description, "has been interwoven under the bird's beak." She seemed oblivious of Lucy's pallor as she picked the object before her up. "And," continued the governor, lifting it clear of her desk, "suspended from the whole thing are a row of teeth."

As the teeth fell downwards in an unseemly fringe beneath the square of grey grass matting, Lucy Durmast's reaction scaled fresh heights of non-verbal communication.

She fainted.

TWELVE

Pulveres—Powders

It was always interesting, decided Detective Inspector Sloan, to meet someone for the second time—if only to check that one's recollection of the first meeting still stood.

Ronald Bolsover was brisker in his office than he had been at home, but this came as no surprise to Sloan, whose own pace slowed down too as he crossed his domestic threshold. All the modern appliances of efficiency were there in the office as well and they made for a certain quickening of tempo. So did the fact that the occupants were visible—even if not audible—to the rest of the office. It would be a self-confident man who sat back and twiddled his thumbs at Ronald Bolsover's desk in full view of the rest of the staff.

Not that Bolsover appeared to hurry either. Here was a deliberate, careful character, probably the ideal anchorman to a restless energetic chairman. Every born leader needed a patient number two and Ronald Bolsover might well be the natural consolidator, the sort of man you did leave to hold the fort. He waved both policemen into chairs and looked expectantly at Sloan.

"Just a few routine points, sir," said the detective inspector easily. "About things we didn't know about when we saw you before."

"That sounds hopeful." Bolsover cocked his head alertly.

Sloan wasn't sure if hopeful was the word he would have chosen himself. He wasn't even sure where hope came in in a murder investigation. That truth will out, perhaps, but he wasn't absolutely sure about that. There was a German proverb he had heard somewhere about the truth sometimes being too sad to be borne. He cleared his throat and asked more mundanely if Bolsover could tell them anything more about the official opening of the Palshaw Tunnel.

The deputy chairman of Durmast's grimaced. "As a public-relations exercise, which it was meant to be, it was a disaster of magnitude one. There are no two ways about that. Nobody could get the Press to take an interest in anything except the demonstration." He moved to an intercom. "I'll get the prints brought in."

Sloan nodded, not without sympathy, and said, "That would be a help."

"And then when the police started to put a stop to it all the newspapers wanted to do was to photograph the police tangling with the demonstrators."

Detective Constable Crosby stirred, and said morosely, "That's always good for a laugh." He'd been on the front line himself and knew.

"I see," said Sloan to Bolsover. Responses to protests were very nearly as significant as the protests themselves; Sloan was aware of that from experience.

"The Minister was particularly put out," said Bolsover, "as of course the Department of Transport were involved in the funding, though not in the actual work. The County Council organised that."

"Quite so," said Sloan, although in fact local authority finance was almost a closed book to him. Other, better men than he, lost sleep over the precept for policing the County of Calleshire and the Rate Support Grant.

"The Lord Lieutenant was naturally all for carrying on regardless," said Bolsover.

"Naturally," echoed Sloan. Put into Latin and the sentiment would have done for the family motto of the Dukes of Calleshire. Carrying on regardless was what His Grace's family had been doing since time out of mind. Predictably the only ribbons that cut any ice with the Duke were either Garter ones or faded mementos of wars well fought, worn of the left breast: one in front of a tunnel wouldn't carry much weight with His Grace. One man's mob, though, was another man's protest group and—more important perhaps—another man's constituents.

"The chairman of the Calleshire County Council wasn't exactly happy either," said Bolsover.

"And Mr. Durmast?" asked Sloan curiously.

"Bill?" Bolsover gave a short laugh. "Oh, Bill wasn't too worried. Like the old trouper he is he insisted that all publicity is good publicity. He told us to wait until the tunnel collapsed before we complained about bad publicity. When that happened he said we could shout as much as we liked. He always said when we did have any little problems to look at Brunel."

"What about when all your troubles weren't little ones?" asked Crosby.

"Then," replied Bolsover, "he would say not to forget the Tay Bridge and what happened to that."

"Ah," said Sloan. The chairman's approach went a long way towards explaining how it was that Bill Durmast got on well with Hamish Mgambo and King Thabile III.

"That quietened Clopton's," said Bolsover. "They were the contractors."

"I expect it did," said Sloan.

"But it was a disappointment all the same," he admitted.

"The demonstrators . . ."

"Oh, you people caught some of them," said Bolsover, "but that wasn't the point. It wasn't revenge we were after. Besides"—he shrugged his shoulders—"they came up in front of old Pussyfoot."

"Who?"

"Henry Simmonds of Almstone."

"The Chairman of the Berebury Bench, you mean?"

"Mr. Softie himself," said Bolsover.

"We knock 'em off," chorussed Crosby cheerfully, "the probation officer gets 'em off and the Bench lets 'em off."

"They pushed an open door," said Sloan with legal literalness.

"Exactly," agreed Bolsover, adding with a touch of bitterness, "the Law apparently takes a different view of trespass when a door is open."

"Question," enquired Crosby of nobody in particular, "when is a door not a door? Answer: when it's a jar."

"Who opened the door?" asked Sloan, rising above the interruption.

"Wish we knew," said Bolsover, "but we don't. Nobody knows. The protesters must have had a sympathiser on site somewhere but we never found out who."

"Kenneth Carline?" Sloan trawled the name in front of Bolsover without inflection.

"I didn't know him as anti-nuclear," said Bolsover slowly, "but you can't always tell, can you? He played a lot of Rugby . . . oh, thank you, Mary. These are the photographs, Inspector . . ."

The remark about the Rugby was neither a non sequiteur nor evidence, but Detective Inspector Sloan, working policeman, knew what Bolsover meant. Caesar Lombroso might have been the first man after William Shakespeare to wonder about the link between physical make-up and crime but he certainly wasn't the last. Sloan was only too well aware that most of the criminals he apprehended were small, thin men. Perhaps there was a corollary: that even ways of thought were after all linked to physical make-up. That would inch the answer to crime nearer still to where he, Sloan, thought it belonged—not with the psychiatrists and sociologists but with the biochemists.

He turned to the press cuttings that Ronald Bolsover had handed to him. This was no time for theorising.

The Calleford newspaper had done the protesters well. Their main picture was of an enormous banner extending right across the width of the Palshaw Tunnel mouth like a gigantic tympanun. It proclaimed: "Nuclear Waste Damages Your Health." Underneath that was a photograph of two large policemen apparently felling a defenceless young girl unprovoked. There were sundry other views of the protest crowd above the tunnel opening and a file portrait of the Lord Lieutenant of Calleshire, His Grace the Duke of Calleshire, taken on some other quite unrelated occasion. They also portrayed the unavailing attempt of Sergeant Watkinson to assail the group from below. A later photograph showed him being carried to an ambulance . . .

The text was as loaded as the photographs. The reporter managed a mention of the length of the tunnel in metres but that was about all. It was obvious that the press hand-out from Durmast's had been passed over in favour of suggestions that the tunnel itself might have a nuclear bunker concealed in its underwater workings. The chairman of William Durmast had stoutly denied this in an interview with a staff reporter but he got two column inches of newsprint compared with Melissa Wainwright's seven and a half column inches of implication and allegation.

Bill Durmast's attempt to expand on the technical difficulties of constructing a tunnel, let alone an extraneous nuclear shelter, in Lower Greensand under Gault were glossed over. So was his vig-

orous comment that he wasn't technically competent to do such
work. Anyone whose first structural-engineering project, he had
said to an inattentive newspaperman, had been doing the hand
digging for an Anderson Shelter at the bottom of the garden at the
outbreak of the Second World War at the age of eleven was too old
to be thinking in terms of preparing for the next one.

"It was all very well for Bill to shrug off the opening," said
Bolsover, "but, dammit, we'd just built a tunnel that everyone had
wanted for years and years."

"I gather," ventured Sloan, "that that is more than can be said
about Durmast's current undertaking."

"Mgongwala?" Bolsover looked up sharply. "What about
Mgongwala?"

Sloan cleared his throat. "It doesn't appear to have unanimous
support either."

"What does?" Ronald Bolsover raised his eyebrows heaven-
wards. "I've never met anything that everyone was pleased about
—let alone a civil-engineering project."

"Prince Aturu is against, we understand."

"So Carline told us," growled Bolsover. "I advised him to watch
his step with that young man. Too clever for his own good is
Prince Aturu. Actually Bill and I both warned Kenneth Carline
about having anything to do with Dlasian politics even on the
sidelines."

"And you don't think he did?"

The deputy chairman paused for thought. "I really don't know
for certain. He said he couldn't very well stop seeing the Prince
altogether, as they'd known each other quite well at university and
nothing would stop Aturu from talking politics when they did
meet . . ."

Politicians had a lot in common, thought Sloan to himself.

"So it wouldn't have been easy," retailed Bolsover, "but he did
promise to be especially careful about meeting Aturu until after
Commenda. Only, of course, Kenneth was killed and so it didn't
arise."

"Commenda?" Sloan queried a word he didn't know.

"That's Dlasa's great festival of the year," said Bolsover. "When
they have the ceremony of dismissing unfriendly spirits. King
Thabile comes out of his palace dressed in his ancestor's clothes
and bids them go."

"I see," said Sloan. Many years ago an infant Christopher Dennis Sloan had been christened in a gown first used at his great grandmother's christening service but that, he supposed, was rather different.

"He's a hereditary monarch, of course," said Bolsover.

"So the clothes should fit," remarked Crosby irreverently.

At their wedding Sloan's wife, Margaret, had worn her mother's veil . . .

Ronald Bolsover's mind was working on quite a different tack. "I understand from Bill that Dlasian spirit gods are very nearly as unpredictable as our local planning committees."

Sloan made sympathetic noises.

"And," swept on Bolsover, "that the Dlasian system of waiting until the auguries are right is even more complicated than our Town and Country Planning Acts, which I must say some might find it difficult to believe . . ."

"Did you know the Prince?"

"Not really." The deputy chairman shook his head. "He came into the office here once or twice to see Ken but we soon put a stop to that. There's too much riding on the Mgongwala contract for social niceties."

"Of course," responded Sloan aloud.

What he would dearly have liked to have known was whether there was enough riding on the Mgongwala contract for murder.

"But what did they come for?" asked John Allsworthy, settling down beside his own fireside in the Manor House at Brattle Episcopi as evening drew in. Here was an older building by far than the Queen Anne Old Rectory that belonged to Bill Durmast.

Cecelia Allsworthy wrinkled her brow. "I don't really know."

"The same two who came before?"

"Oh yes. Inspector Sloan and Constable Crosby."

"Curious," said John Allsworthy, stretching out his long legs in front of the fire, "that they should come back a second time."

"That's what I thought, too," said his wife soberly.

"They didn't say why they came back, I suppose?"

"No."

"Not even," he enquired carefully, "that they had found out something new?"

She shook her head.

"They must have had a reason."

"I know."

"Funny, all the same," he said after a pause.

"What could there have been new anyway?" she asked.

"I don't know." He frowned. "You never can tell. Sherry?"

"Thank you, darling." She sat down on the chair opposite him. There was no sign of the potter's smock or working jeans in the drawing room. Cecelia had on a fine wool dress in a soft pattern of subdued reds and blues with a contrasting plain white collar. "Dinner won't be long."

"It must be Thursday," said John Allsworthy suddenly. "No Hortense."

"She's gone to a French film in Calleford," replied Cecelia. "She was meeting her pal Clémence first and going with her. She won't be home until the last bus, so remember not to bolt the front door, darling, won't you?"

"An evening to ourselves," he said luxoriously.

"At the rate they're growing," said their mother, "the twins will be staying up for dinner any day now."

"As long as you're here," said her husband uxoriously, "I have no complaints at all." He extended his arm round her shoulders. Presently he said, "It's been a long day."

Cecelia Allsworthy immediately projected a proper wifely interest and listened with close attention while he told her about it. John Allsworthy never asked her about her work, and for this—artist that she was—she was grateful. When, on the rare occasions she did volunteer that it had gone well or ill, he confined himself to the two stock responses considered the ideal between partners at the bridge table: "Well done" and "Bad luck."

John Allsworthy said, "Hawkins says that all the fences down at Birdler's Bottom are going to need renewing soon. That'll cost a pretty penny."

"That reminds me," said Cecelia, "the Parish Council want to Beat the Bounds next month."

He grunted. "I must remember to check on that beer barrel in the cellar then."

"I tried to explain to Hortense that it was a revival of the ancient custom of making sure that the next generation knew where the parish boundaries were before maps . . ."

"By banging their heads on a stone," he added amiably. "I hope you didn't forget that bit. It's how we perfidious Albions give youngsters a bump of locality."

". . . But I don't think she really understood," said Cecelia. "They must have a different system in France. She didn't even know what a bump of locality was until I explained."

"At least we'd got going on parish boundaries before the Normans came over," said the Squire of Braffle Episcopi.

"Not county ones, though," she said mischievously. "They're Norman, aren't they?"

"They were," he grumbled, "until we had all that local government reorganisation." Mercifully the county of Calleshire had emerged intact, if not exactly unscathed, from the reforms of the Redcliffe-Maud Commission. John Allsworthy had a cousin in the West Riding of Yorkshire who was still inclined to wax eloquent on this.

"And," continued Cecelia Allsworthy, "the rector called. He's having another crisis of conscience about Lucy. He's still worried in case he ought to be getting in touch with Bill Durmast."

"She won't thank him for it, if he does," said Allsworthy, "and I've told him so."

"I tried to explain to him about the importance the Dlasians attach to this Festival of the Departure of the Unfriendly Spirits of theirs, and how we're so sure that Lucy wouldn't want Bill worried at least until it's safely over—but I don't think he took it really seriously."

"Professional jealousy," said her spouse unfeelingly.

"By the way, he also came to ask you to read the Lesson on Sunday."

"First or Second?"

"Second."

"That's a relief. Trying to say 'Ahasuerus' before the assembled congregation always unnerves me and amuses everyone else. Remind me to check the Lectionary."

"John!"

"Can't be too careful with the Church anti-militant," said her husband unrepentantly. "I'm sure he once did me out of reading that nice piece on army recruitment by Gideon."

"Don't be silly."

"Moreover," carried on Allsworthy, "I think he's afraid the congregation can't hear the difference between warmonger and whoremonger. I never get to read anything like that since he's been in office . . ."

It wasn't the pronouncing of the names of Old Testament Kings or ancient vices that was worrying Cecelia Allsworthy. "John, there was one rather odd thing that those policemen did want to know that did rather bother me."

He looked up, quite serious now. "What was that?"

"Whether or not Lucy was interested in nuclear disarmament."

"Lucy?"

"That's what they asked."

"But why Lucy?" he said. "If it's anyone they should be asking, its . . ."

"Exactly." Husband and wife exchanged one of those looks of total understanding that can pass only between married couples. Cecelia rose. "Finish your sherry slowly, darling, will you, and then come through."

THIRTEEN

Conspersi—Dusting-powders

Detective Inspector Sloan also eventually reached his own home and waiting wife, although much too late for his son to lisp his sire's return or for Sloan himself to be even momentarily cheered by the sight of "this fair child of mine." He had found "To be new-made when thou art old" one of the deepest feelings he had experienced in his own particular "forty winters" of Shakespeare's sonnet on parenthood.

A lesser domestic matter came to the forefront of his consciousness as he walked up the garden path to his own front door, determinedly trying to put the case of Lucy Durmast out of his mind as he did so. The problem was simple. He, Christopher Dennis Sloan, quondam gardener, would dearly have liked to plant an old-fashioned climbing rose—say Gloire de Dijon—at the far side of the sitting-room window to go with the Paul Léde that was doing so well round the porch. He was constrained from so doing though by the thought of the reaction of Peter Hamilton.

The Hamiltons were good neighbours—the proverbial cup of sugar was always available when urgently needed—and the Sloans were on the best of terms with them. Nevertheless of late Sloan had begun to detect a certain reserve in Peter Hamilton's admiration of his next-door neighbour's prize roses.

Sloan knew what had done it.

Last year he had grown to perfection for the very first time a really stunning Sandringham Centenary—a tall rose of rich burnt-copper colouring: had taken first prize with it too at the Berebury Horticultural Summer Show.

Unfortunately Peter Hamilton on his side of the fence had failed miserably to get his solitary bush of Whisky Mac to do at all well: had even let it get greenfly.

It was only a lifetime's training in the discipline of measured and orderly response to provocation that had enabled Sloan to refrain from commenting on the greenfly. He had even waited to give his own precious bushes a precautionary spray until his neighbour was at work, finding some hidden serendipity in the shift system as he did so.

Even Sloan was aware that Peter Hamilton was beginning to be resentful about all that was good about his garden. Peter hadn't even asked Sloan for advice on his failing Karl Druschki, which the policeman took to be a bad sign. Yet he couldn't possibly keep down a strong climbing tea rose like Gloire de Dijon—very free flowering the catalogue said—even if he did plant it by the sitting-room window, and the more attention he gave to the rather rarer Paul Léde over the porch the more splendid it became. He couldn't even put the Gloire de Dijon at the back of the house, because he'd got Vicomtesse Pierre de Fou there and doing very well round the kitchen door.

He—Sloan—had once even gone as far as mentioning the dilemma he felt himself to be in to his friend Happy Harry, Berebury Division's Traffic Inspector.

There had been no comfort to be had in that quarter.

"Policemen don't have friends," Inspector Harpe had sniffed.

"I suppose not," Sloan had responded with a certain melancholy.

"And," the traffic man had added pertinently, "neither, come to that, do gardeners who grow for show. You ought to know that by now, Seedy."

Detective Inspector Sloan braced his shoulders this evening and went indoors prepared to try to put the cares and burdens of the day and of his garden behind him.

He couldn't, of course.

By the time he was outside a good helping of beef stew and well into an excellent plum tart—nobody he knew had a lighter hand with pastry than Margaret—he was telling her about the strange message—if that was what it was—that Lucy Durmast had been sent at the prison.

"I thought," said Margaret Sloan, "that Trevor Porritt had said that the murder was all about a love affair that had gone wrong. Not about Africa."

"He did," said Sloan, "and there's nothing to prove it wasn't."

He paused and thought awhile. "Nothing at all. That's the funny thing. Except that she's still not saying anything."

"Perhaps she hasn't anything to say," suggested Margaret Sloan placidly.

"She could at least say she isn't guilty," said Sloan with the sort of irritability that can only be given free expression in the home, "if she isn't."

"I don't see why she should," responded his wife with feminine logic, "since she knows perfectly well that you're not going to believe her anyway."

"She could still tell us why she . . ."

"And there's another thing to consider." Margaret edged a dish of homemade custard in his direction. "If she knows she didn't do it, she might not care all that much whether anyone else knows or not."

"She doesn't look a 'damn your eyes' sort of girl."

"It's what you think of yourself that matters, you know, in the long run." She frowned. "That's why it's the things that injure your image of yourself—scars and that sort of thing—count so much."

Sloan addressed himself to the plum tart and custard while he considered this.

"Moreover," continued his wife, warming to her theme, "she also may know that anything she does say may only make matters worse."

He nodded. He knew what she was thinking. Once, quite early in their married life, Sloan had taken her to the old Calleford Assizes to see a famous Queen's Counsel in action. Unfortunately the experience had only strengthened her convictions that the Law was an ass. The Q.C.'s interrogation of a hostile but perfectly truthful witness had only impressed her by its apparent total unfairness.

"This African message," she said. "What is it exactly?"

"Nobody knows," said her husband. "It's being copied and sent over from Cottingham Grange for me to see. It doesn't," he added fairly, "mean that Lucy Durmast didn't kill Kenneth Carline. In fact, if Prince Aturu sent it, whatever it is, it could be because Lucy had killed his friend Kenneth. After all, for all I know they may think differently about justice and revenge in Dlasa."

"I daresay they do," rejoined his wife drily. "And who's to say who's right?"

"We don't even know what it means," he said, ducking that issue. "Drawings like hieroglyphics the governor said, only she didn't have a Rosetta Stone handy at the prison." The governor of Cottingham Grange was a woman with a finely attuned sense of humour, which was just as well, since it wasn't everyone's choice of career. "All we know is that Lucy Durmast fainted when she saw it."

"I'm not surprised," said Margaret Sloan warmly.

"Or pretended to faint," added Sloan from a long habit of caution.

"The governor would know which," said Margaret Sloan, undeterred. "At least Lucy Durmast was entitled to think she would be safe from that sort of thing in prison."

"Well . . ." A place of safety was the term used for the building or institution where those in need of care and attention were taken by order of a benevolent government, but Detective Inspector Sloan wasn't so naïve as to think that prisons came into that category. The Act of Parliament in question was referring to hospitals. People were sent to prison on an order for the governor to have and to hold . . . That reminded him of something else. He looked his wife straight in the eye and said, "Would you have killed me if I'd got engaged to someone else?"

"No," she said without hesitation.

"Well, then . . ."

"But I might have killed myself." She held a dish out. "More tart?"

"We've come about the Kingdom of Dlasa," said Detective Inspector Sloan the next morning to the smooth young man sitting behind his desk in his office on the fourth floor of the Ministry for Overseas Development.

It was quite a nice desk in its way but nothing like as elegant a one as that in the government department that the two policemen had just left. That had been the Foreign and Commonwealth Office. The men from Calleshire had been treated there with great courtesy and attention and, with a skill born of long practice, immediately passed on to another department. It was not for nothing that the first Secretary of State at the Foreign Office had been the wily Charles James Fox. Sloan, who had noticed a bust of the famous politician in the entrance hall, knew gamekeepers living deep in the heart of rural Calleshire who still called foxes "Mister Charles" in tribute to the great cunning of both animals—Fox, the man, and fox—*Vulpes vulpes*—the creature of the wild.

"It's in Africa," added Detective Constable Crosby helpfully.

Sloan didn't enjoy coming up to London but he had felt that his mission of enquiry about Dlasa could not be accomplished on his behalf by a friendly officer from the Metropolitan Police, however well briefed. For one thing, that officer might legitimately feel that the Calleshire Force was a little short of hard evidence on which to base their enquiries. There was another reason, too, for Berebury Division to make its own mistakes. Sloan didn't want any laughs by the Met at the expense of bucolic bumpkins up from the country with straws showing in their hair: the superintendent was very sensitive about that sort of thing.

Or, if it came to that, any amusement exhibited by high-flying young civil servants confronted by a constable of the calibre of Dogberry and Virges either.

"Indeed yes," diplomatically responded James Jeavington, the civil servant, to Detective Constable Crosby. He was, in fact, the Ministry's Dlasian specialist. "In Africa. Precisely. The Dark Continent."

"We need a little background to the present situation in Dlasa," explained Sloan hastily, "and we understand that you would be the best people to help us."

"Naturally," said Jeavington fluently, "my Ministry would wish to be as constructive as possible."

Sloan let that pass.

"In what way, though, can Overseas Development be of assistance to the Calleshire Constabulary?" asked the civil servant.

"We would like to know something about the contract for the building of Mgongwala."

James Jeavington at once projected extreme caution. "What about it exactly, Inspector?"

"For instance," said Sloan, "how it was awarded."

"It went to Durmast's, the civil-engineering people from . . ." His voice changed suddenly and he added in quite a different tone ". . . from Calleford." He paused. "I see."

Detective Inspector Sloan hunched his shoulders. "A junior

member of the firm of Durmast's was friendly with one of the sons of the King of Dlasa—Prince Aturu—who has been a dedicated opponent of the building of the new town at Mgongwala."

Jeavington looked extremely alert but not surprised.

"The member of the firm," said Sloan succinctly, "with whom Prince Aturu was friendly has been murdered and we understand that the Prince has been recalled to Dlasa. We need to know if there is any connection at all between these two events."

"I see," said Jeavington slowly.

"How did Durmast's get the contract in the first instance?" Sloan came back to his original question.

James Jeavington paused for so long before he answered him that Sloan began to wonder if the Ministry was a punishment station for failed Treasury men. "I think," he said at last, "that it would be fair to say that they had won it."

"In fair combat?"

"Everything is fair in international dealing, Inspector."

"Like love and war," said Crosby brightly.

"By sealed tender, for example?" persisted Sloan.

Jeavington shook his head. "Seals can be opened and resealed." That much every administrator knew.

"By open tender, then?" suggested Sloan.

The civil servant avoided his gaze. "I think it would be—er—unwise of you to assume that that was the method by which Durmast's got the job."

"And naïve?"

"Durmast's is a firm with a very good reputation."

"There are a great many civil-engineering firms with good reputations," rejoined Sloan.

"Her Majesty's Government was anxious that the work should be done by a firm from the United Kingdom."

"I'll bet," said Detective Constable Crosby inelegantly.

"Besides which, Inspector . . ." added Jeavington.

"Yes?"

"In some respects the African mind works rather differently from the occidental one."

"Cricket," said Sloan, "doesn't come into it, is that what you mean?"

"I do not think," said Jeavington, "that Hamish Mgambo was

ever a man to be influenced by breathless hushes in the close to-
night or any night."

"And King Thabile?"

"The only things," pronounced Jeavington a little acidly, "that
would appear to influence King Thabile III of Dlasa are the afore-
mentioned Hamish Mgambo and a certain well-known provision
store in Piccadilly."

Sloan lifted an enquiring eyebrow.

"The King," explained Jeavington, "has a great partiality for a
special variety of chocolate biscuit."

"It's like the Criminal Record Office, isn't it?" broke in Detective
Constable Crosby chattily. "Your knowing everyone's weaknesses
and writing it all down."

"And strengths." Jeavington didn't contest the point, only amplified it. "They're just as important."

Detective Inspector Sloan had once been to a lecture on man
management. All that he remembered about it now had been the
aphorism "Build on strength: don't undermine weakness." It
would be difficult to apply to Crosby.

"We make a note of strengths too," the constable was saying now
quite eagerly to the civil servant. "Know your enemy and all that."

"Dlasa's a friendly state," said Jeavington mildly. "Queen Victoria sent the Prince of Wales there on a state visit and King
Thabile's grandfather came over for King Edward's Coronation in
1902."

"And what are Dlasa's strengths?" asked Sloan with genuine
curiosity.

"A rather Edwardian attitude to Europe, a self-sufficient food
supply . . ."

"Except for chocolate biscuits," put in Crosby.

"Our envoy always takes a case of them when he presents his
credentials."

"Envoy?" Sloan picked up a word he wasn't absolutely sure
about.

"A minister plenipotentiary," explained Jeavington fluently.

"What's that?"

"A public minister sent by one sovereign to another for the
transaction of diplomatic business."

"Not an ambassador?" queried Sloan.

"Ranking below an ambassador . . ."

"I see."

". . . but above a chargé d'affaires."

"Either way," Sloan summed up neatly, an old saying coming back to him, "he's a man sent to lie abroad for the good of his country."

The civil servant bowed his head in agreement.

"There was something else we hoped you would be able to tell us about," said Sloan.

"What's that, Inspector?"

Sloan produced a sketch of the missive that had been sent to Lucy Durmast in H. M. Prison Cottingham Grange. "It came under plain cover so to speak." He didn't go into detail about the exhaustive examination of one ordinary envelope, postmarked Calleford, that had yielded no other clues at all about its source.

"That," declared Jeavington without hesitation, "is a Dlasian revenge token."

"We wondered," said Sloan.

"There's the Bird of Disaster—Ahianmworo—in the right-hand corner. Do you see?"

Sloan nodded.

"Highly representational, of course, but no doubt about it. And" —Jeavington pointed to the dangling teeth—"in the Dlasian ethos those represent punishment. The Jaws of Death so to speak."

Crosby stirred uneasily. "Not like that here, is it?"

"You will also have observed the sword of life and death in the other corner."

Crosby said, "There's one of those at the Old Bailey."

"Recipients," remarked James Jeavington with a scholar's detachment, "are meant to turn their faces to the wall and die when they see one of those."

Crosby suddenly became the very embodiment of John Bull. "What? Without a proper trial?"

"Vengeance is mine, saith the Lord Chancellor," murmured Sloan with irony.

"They usually do die, of course," continued Jeavington dispassionately, "and quite quickly too."

"No appeal either," said Crosby who usually thought appeals a waste of valuable police time.

"A sort of fatal inanition sets in." Jeavington looked up. "Did you know that they don't have any prisons in Dlasa?"

"No," said Sloan, suddenly very anxious that Lucy Durmast didn't turn her face to the wall while they were making their enquiries. That wouldn't do at all.

"This hex . . ." began Crosby.

"Yes?" said Jeavington.

"Does it last forever?"

Jeavington shook his head. "Only until the next Festival of Commenda."

"We've heard about that," said Sloan.

"The great Dlasian ceremony of dismissing the Unfriendly Spirits acts as a sort of slate-wiping exercise all round." The civil servant waved a hand. "We could do with one in the Ministry from time to time."

"So," said Crosby seriously, "if the accused can keep going until then she might be all right?"

Jeavington gave a faint smile. "That rather depends on what she has been accused of, doesn't it?"

"And by whom," added Sloan. A Dlasian revenge token was one thing, a warrant issued by an English Court was quite another. Even so, to Sloan, the two together somehow smacked of double jeopardy.

"There's one thing you can be quite sure about the celebration of Commenda," said Jeavington, "and that is that King Thabile won't cut the first turf, so to speak, for Mgongwala until the festival is over and the Unfriendly Spirits dismissed for the year . . ."

Crosby interrupted him. "Have you heard the one about the surgeon doing the first operation in a new hospital theatre?"

"No," said a fascinated Jeavington. "Tell me . . ."

Nothing loath, the constable carried on. "Well, the surgeon handed the scalpel to his assistant and said, 'Here, you cut the first . . .'"

"Crosby!" thundered Sloan.

"Sorry, sir."

"They still go in for apotrophism in Dlasa, of course," James Jeavington picked up the conversation again with practised smoothness. A minister could be even more jejune any day than a police constable.

"What's that when it's at home?" asked Crosby, trying to write the word down.

"The burying of bones under the threshold of a new building to ward off bad luck would be a good example of apotrophism. It is usually," the civil servant added astringently, "at home but not in this instance."

"Bit primitive, isn't it?" said Crosby.

"Practised very widely in England until the seventeenth century," said Jeavington. "Mind you, it's not all that long ago that they used to leave the north door of a church open during a baptism so that evil spirits could leave. That's why it's called the Devil's Door . . ."

"What sort of bones exactly?" asked Sloan carefully, anxious to get something clear. "You're not talking about human sacrifice, are you?" A dissident son was almost too tailor-made for that part: there had never been any suggestion that Abraham hadn't loved Isaac.

"No," said Jeavington. "They gave that up in a sort of Diamond Jubilee tribute to Queen Victoria."

"I'm very glad to hear it," said Sloan earnestly. Propitiating ancient gods, getting auguries right and casting entrails—even consulting astrologers—were all in their way perfectly proper activities for those who believed in them, but the ritual sacrifice of human beings was murder in Sloan's book if not in everyone else's.

"Talking of Queens . . ." Jeavington cleared his throat.

"Yes?" Sloan was all attention.

The civil servant became suddenly circumlocutory. "I think it might not be—er—out of order for me to give you some indication that . . ."

"Yes?" Sloan was even more encouraging.

"My Ministry have it in mind—provided, of course, that all goes well with the building of Mgongwala . . ."

"Of course."

"To recommend the chairman of William Durmast for inclusion in the New Year Honours."

"That'll be a real feather in his cap," responded Sloan without thinking from where that particular expression had come.

"I wonder," said Crosby idly, "what King Thabile will give him if it doesn't go well. The Order of the Boot, I expect."

"Kingship in Dlasa is Divine," said Jeavington seriously, "so it's difficult to say."

Not for the first time Sloan anathematised himself for not paying more attention at school. Wasn't that what all the fuss about King Charles I had been?

"But," swept on Jeavington, "in case you're thinking that Dlasa's backward, let me tell you about the other strength that it has got."

"What's that?" In Detective Inspector Sloan's line of country it was usually weaknesses that were talked about.

"A refreshing absence of civil insurrection." James Jeavington straightened a blotter that ornamented his desk as if ink—real ink —were still in daily use at the Ministry for Overseas Development. "Even though there is a subject race there—the Thecats." He brightened. "Perhaps that explains it. Makes for better behaviour all round, I mean. *Pas devant les domestiques* and all that. I hadn't thought of it in that way." He cocked his head alertly. "Make an interesting study, that, wouldn't it?" The hidden academic in him surfaced briefly.

"Have you any reason to suppose," put in Sloan before the man opposite could expand his hypothesis any further, "that Prince Aturu—er—had it in mind"—two could use the language of diplomacy—"to upset the status quo?"

"Our man in Dlasa," advanced Jeavington obliquely, "has reported that the preparations for the building of Mgongwala appear to be going well, and that there are no signs of imminent destabilisation." He waved a hand. "And he would know. He's worked all over Africa."

"And Prince Aturu?" enquired Sloan. "Has he any news of the Prince since his return from England?"

"It is not, of course, Her Majesty's Envoy's province to monitor the movement of members of the Dlasian Royal family . . ."

"Naturally," agreed Sloan, "but . . ."

"But he can report that nothing whatsoever has been seen of Prince Aturu since he returned to Dlasa . . ."

"Ah."

"If he ever did," said James Jeavington.

FOURTEEN

Collyria—The eye lotions

"Home, James," said Detective Inspector Sloan thankfully as they came out of the Ministry for Overseas Development, "and don't spare the horses." Whitehall was no place for a pair of investigating officers.

He had strapped himself into the passenger seat of the police car before he realised he didn't really mean what he had said. Getting home quickly was the instinctive reaction of the countryman visiting London, that was all: a sentiment as old as Aesop. He turned to Detective Constable Crosby, who was already in the driving seat and added, "Mind you, that's not a licence to kill."

"With this sort of traffic," retorted Crosby morosely, "blood pressure'll be the only thing that kills anyone. Not speed."

"A little time to think won't hurt us." Sloan was at his most bracing.

"Won't do us any good," said Crosby, insinuating the police car into a moving stream of traffic with a truly urban disregard for other drivers. "That pinstripe wonder didn't tell us a lot, did he?"

"Not really." Police Superintendent Leeyes, who didn't have a high opinion of either the city or the civil service, would be sitting at his rather more functional desk in Berebury police station waiting to hear how his two minions had got on. Sloan was only too well aware without Crosby's rubbing it in that there was precious little to tell him.

"Getting nowhere fast," pronounced Crosby, "that's what we're doing."

"It's not for want of trying, is it?" said Sloan drily. "The fast bit, I mean."

Where Crosby appeared to be going fast was an Accident and Emergency Unit. He was engaged in the simultaneous circumnavigation of a London bus and the thwarting of the energetic efforts of a hackney carriage to overtake their car.

"He's probably got a fare with a train to catch," said Sloan absently. They had only got a murderer to catch—no, that had been a Freudian slip. They had caught their murderer, hadn't they? And Detective Inspector Porritt had arrested her. What they were trying to do was collect evidence—no, that was wrong, too. They had got their evidence, hadn't they? He took hold of his thoughts. What was it that everyone was shouting about then?

First, identify the problem: that was what all the good books said.

Detective Inspector Sloan shrank back in the front passenger seat and tried to put the Law's problem into words.

A girl who had chosen to stay silent in Court.

A rational Sloan reminded himself that a great many accused persons chose not to give evidence at their own trials and that did not seem in any way seriously to upset the balance of the Scales of Justice: it wasn't all that long ago that they hadn't even been allowed to—whether or not they wished to.

"That sword at the Old Bailey," he said suddenly to an uninterested detective constable at the driving wheel, "isn't like the Dlasian one." They'd had a talk once on the history of the Law at one of the courses that Sloan had been sent on. It was funny which bits surfaced from time to time. "It isn't called the Sword of Life or Death like theirs."

Crosby changed the gears down suddenly for a quick spurt of speed.

"It's called the Sword of Mercy or Curtana."

"Chap I knew," remarked Crosby laconically, "told me it was pointless."

"Hasn't got a point." Sloan rephrased the description. *Double entendre* was all very well in its place but not with Crosby. "It's blunt." Perhaps, now he came to think about it, that was better in every way than its being two-edged, like the Dlasian one.

Life or death, Jeavington had said, hadn't he?

And infinitely more merciful for it to be blunt than sharp.

What he really needed to know was exactly where the Kingdom of Dlasa—whatever sort of sword it used in its symbolism—came into the murder of Kenneth Carline.

If it did.

Sloan tried to relax. "There's probably quite a simple explanation for everything if we did but know," he said aloud.

"I don't know where that truck thinks it's going," said Crosby, "but . . ."

"Lucy Durmast," Sloan pressed on sturdily, "might only have wanted to delay her trial until after the Festival of the Departure of the Unfriendly Spirits was safely over."

"Shouldn't be on the road," said Crosby indignantly as the driver of the truck executed a neat *pas de deux* with a sports car. The owner of the sports car had youth as well as speed on his side and was soon almost out of sight. "I'd book him if we were in Calleshire . . ."

"That," said Sloan with commendable pertinacity, "would have at least have got her father and Mgongwala off to a good start."

"And got William Durmast his gong," said Crosby, losing interest in the truck.

"It would be salvaging something," said Sloan moderately.

Crosby screwed his neck round, craning to see behind him. They were still leading the taxi by a short head.

"And account for Lucy Durmast's silence," said Sloan.

Crosby sniffed. "It could be that she isn't saying anything because she hasn't anything to say."

That had been what Margaret Sloan had said too. Sloan advanced another stray thought that he had had. "I think we can presume," he said, "that Lucy Durmast isn't likely to take any action that would injure the firm of Durmast. Quite apart from anything else, she's got a sizeable stake in it, remember? Her late mother's holding as well as her own, Inspector Porritt put in his report."

"Sacrificing her chances with a jury in a good cause?" Crosby frowned. "Doesn't make sense to me."

"Some women," said Sloan wisely, "will always go in for self-sacrifice. It's in the nature of the beast or something. You've got to watch them."

Crosby increased his lead on the taxi before he spoke. "All that about the firm doesn't go for Kenneth Carline though, does it?"

"We don't know," said Sloan. In his book Lucy Durmast's considerable holding in the firm was a powerful reason for courting the boss's daughter, not for getting engaged to someone else. It wasn't that he was naturally cynical. Once Margaret had dragged

him to a performance by the Berebury Amateur Dramatic Society
of the play *The Heiress* by Henry James. The society was affection-
ately known in the town of Berebury as the BADS and the acting
had been far from memorable, but Sloan had never forgotten the
message in the play.

Crosby sniffed. "You'll always find somebody ready to bite the
hand that feeds them."

"Industrial espionage is on the increase," said Sloan less demoti-
cally.

"Someone with a key," said Crosby, "opened the gate that let the
demonstrators in to where the tunnel is." The taxi-cab had
dropped so far behind as not to be a challenge to his thinking.

"And telephoned to say that the gate would be open . . ."

"With the key in the lock on the inside," Crosby reminded him,
"to keep us out."

"Quite so," said Sloan, intrigued by the detective constable's use
of the word "us." He didn't usually identify himself with the force
at all.

"But mucking up an opening ceremony in Calleshire is hardly
likely to damage a contract in Dlasa, is it, sir?"

"It might only have been . . ." began Sloan and then changed
his tone as a lightning flash of adrenalin coursed through his system. "Mind that lorry!"

"Plenty of room," said Crosby airily.

Sloan hung on to the shreds of his temper with an almost palpa-
ble effort. "Just you remember, Crosby," he said between gritted
teeth, "that it's not only a car that can be recalled by its maker."

"Think they own the road," said Crosby. "That's their trouble."

"Our trouble," said Sloan pertinently, "is that we're not getting
anywhere with an investigation that should have been over and
done with days ago."

"Concrete evidence," said Crosby, "that's what we haven't got,
isn't it?"

"Yet," said Sloan.

"Back to the drawing board?" suggested Crosby. "Do you know,
sir, I'd never seen a real drawing board until we went to see that
fellow Bolsover. He's got proper stand-up jobs there in his office."

"I daresay he needs them," said Sloan absently. It was always
interesting to trace figures of speech back to their origins. Archi-

tects drew standing, didn't they? Like, according to Vespasian, emperors should die.

"Don't know where we'd begin," said Crosby. "It's not like a tunnel, is it, where you've got two ends."

Sloan suspected that even starting a tunnel on paper wasn't as simple as all that. "Myself," he said, "in a murder case I like to begin with the body."

"It's all we've got anyway, sir, isn't it?" said Crosby realistically.

"Very true." There hadn't even been an empty bottle of hyoscine around. Inspector Porritt had searched the Old Rectory at Brattle Episcopi for evidence in vain. "Just a body."

"Rather a bashed one," said Crosby, "what with the car accident and all that."

"Rugby's a rough game at the best of times," murmured Sloan.

"Yes, sir." The games of Detective Constable Crosby's childhood had all been with a round ball. That didn't mean that they had been any the gentler for it, just different.

"I suppose, though," said Sloan, "that what we know about Carline's last weekend begins there. We'd better check on the match in the local paper . . ."

"We know something earlier than that," said Crosby intelligently. The road fore and aft was momentarily clear and he had nothing else to interest him. "On the Friday afternoon the deceased saw Mr. Bolsover and made another appointment with him for the Monday morning."

"So we do." Sloan hitched his shoulders. "We have a timetable, then. That'll give us somewhere to start on a new drawing board." He wondered how many times Trevor Porritt had done this in preparing the case of the Crown *v.* Lucy Mirabel Durmast.

"Friday Carline sees the deputy chairman of the firm."

"Saturday he plays Rugby," said Sloan.

"Sunday he licks his wounds."

"Monday he sees Mr. Bolsover again," said Sloan.

"Has lunch with the accused . . ."

"Crashes his car."

"Taken to hospital."

"Dies," said Sloan succinctly.

"This is the end of Solomon Grundy," chanted Crosby. "Ah, here's our road . . ."

Detective Inspector Sloan decided to try to exercise mind over matter. He deliberately averted his gaze from the way ahead and considered the alleged murder of Kenneth Carline by Lucy Durmast, it was said for reasons of the heart. He had been taught at the Police Training College that there were five natural emotions: fear, grief, anger, jealousy and love. The man who had done the teaching had appeared to be without any of them—dispassionate, colourless, academic. Most of those who had instructed police officers at their training colleges had seemed like that man and yet he had finished his spiel quite unselfconsciously with something very near to parody. "And the greatest of these," he had said, "is love."

If the murder was for any other reason than love there was a conspicuous absence of visible ill-gotten gains. The balance sheet of William Durmast's firm had contained nothing exceptional. A careful Trevor Porritt had checked that early on in his investigation. Inspector Porritt had been a thorough, painstaking officer who hadn't, as far as he could see, overlooked anything that he, Sloan, could think of. And much good being a thorough, painstaking officer had done the poor chap. Sloan bet that Porritt had never dreamt when he went on duty the day of his accident that it was going to be his last in the Force. What was it that the cynics said— the worst case is never envisaged and always encountered.

He tightened his lips subconsciously. Now he was beginning to think like Superintendent Leeyes. That would never do. And yet it was perhaps just this very capacity for looking on the black side that separated the men from the boys. He pulled his thoughts together with a jerk, determined not to let a natural pessimism triumph.

All that was wrong, he told himself firmly, was that there were too many unknown factors in this particular equation which equalled murder. His old maths master would have said "Let x equal the number you don't know" and gone on in his gentle, persuasive way to reason how letting that x equal the unknown factor and y and z represent what you did know, you could work out the value of x in a trice.

Only this time he didn't know what y and z were equal to either, and since they, too, were unknown he couldn't even begin on his equation. Not that he was a mathematician anyway—innumerate, the maths master had called him on his school report. Gentle the teacher might have been, but there were no untruths in mathematics and he saw no reason for equivocation in his comments to

Sloan's father. He'd been right, of course. Even now only Imperial measures really meant anything to Sloan in his mind's eye. It would be all right for those youngsters who had been brought up on the metric system alone—a sort of reverse of "those who only England know . . ."

Perhaps they should be going back to an abacus rather than a drawing board, and yet if money had come into murder, he, Sloan, professional policeman, was blessed if he could see where. True, Ronald Bolsover and Kenneth Carline had been on their way to the Palgrave Tunnel to discuss the handing over of the last of their retention fee to the contractors—Clopton's—for the construction of the tunnel when Carline had come to grief, but a meticulous Trevor Porritt had even checked that out. All the fees had been paid and the completed works duly handed over to the County Surveyor on schedule and the Department of Transport so informed so that it could do its share of the funding.

"It's a pity there's so little in the way of circumstantial evidence," he heard himself saying aloud to the detective constable at his side.

"For or against?"

"That's an interesting point," he said gravely.

"There's that powerfully flavoured stuff Lucy Durmast served him up with," said Crosby, blissfully untroubled by the pedantic positioning of prepositions. "Why did she bother if she hadn't got something to hide?"

"Alimentary, my dear Watson . . ." Sloan allowed himself a measure of unaccustomed latitude.

"Pardon, sir?"

"Nothing."

Crosby swung the steering wheel over and took the fork in the road that would lead them back in due course to the County of Calleshire, and said "Lucy is short for Lucretia."

"I am well aware of that, thank you, Crosby." He turned his attention back to the road ahead. "But if I may say so, it is not a particularly helpful remark at this juncture."

"Sorry, sir." The constable straightened up the wheel.

Detective Inspector Sloan, too, sensed that the city was behind them. He put his notebook into his brief-case. Country mice they might be, but there was no doubt that the city didn't have the solution to their problem.

Whether the African continent did was another matter entirely.

Crosby shared the sentiment. "Funny, sir, though all the same, that fellow Prince Aturu disappearing just when he did."

Sloan couldn't see where Prince Aturu or his departure fitted into the picture at all and said so.

"Perhaps he was afraid he would be the next to die," rejoined the constable, his foot resuming the accelerator.

In spite of their fears, in the event it wasn't Prince Aturu, son of King Thabile the Third of Dlasa, who was the next to die, nor even Detective Inspector C. D. Sloan, Head of the Criminal Investigation Department of the Berebury Division of the Calleshire County Constabulary, unhappy passenger in a fast car.

The first inkling that Sloan had that somebody else might have done so though was when Detective Constable Crosby swung their car into the car park behind the Police Station at Berebury. It was unusually crowded, and standing in the middle of the yard, causing even greater congestion, was the caravan that served variously as an information office, mobile rest room and murder van.

"Something's up," observed Crosby.

"Something big," concluded Sloan. "That's the assistant chief constable's car over there."

To say that Superintendent Leeyes was glad to see the two officers was something of an understatement. "There you are at last, Sloan," he barked. "You can forget the Carline murder for a while. We've got one on our own patch."

"Sir?"

"Body found in a ditch off the Calleford road," he said tersely. "About half an hour ago. Get out there now before anyone else mucks anything about . . ."

"Who?"

"All I know," snapped Leeyes whom sudden death made especially irritable, "is that the victim is young and female."

Sloan nodded sadly. Victims usually were young and female.

"She hasn't been identified yet," Leeyes surged on. "They're waiting until Dr. Dabbe gets there before they touch anything."

It did not occur to Sloan to admonish Crosby about his speed on the journey out of Berebury to a spot just outside the town on the Calleford road and it was in record time that they slid to a halt behind the car belonging to Dr. Dabbe, Consultant Pathologist to the Berebury District General Hospital.

The doctor was down in the ditch, being very careful indeed about where he put his feet. Someone had rigged up a makeshift duckboard for him, but it didn't reach quite far enough.

The body was lying face down in a mixture of grass and water, but Detective Inspector Sloan could see all he needed to from where he stood. He needed neither to go nearer nor to see the girl's face to make an identification: a mottled green skirt and a burgundy-coloured blouse told him all he needed to know. He'd been looking at those very same clothes only yesterday afternoon.

He felt suddenly very tired and disheartened as he called down to Dr. Dabbe, "I don't know her surname, Doctor, but I'm very much afraid that her Christian name is Hortense. She's French . . ."

FIFTEEN

Collutoria—Mouth-washes

"I don't like it, Sloan," snapped Superintendent Leeyes. "I don't like it at all."

"No, sir," said Sloan. That reaction, at least, had been predictable.

"The Allsworthys' *au pair!* You're quite sure, aren't you, Sloan?"

"Quite sure, sir."

"She's dead, of course?"

"No doubt about it, sir, I'm afraid." Detective Inspector Sloan didn't like the murder of Hortense either. He didn't like murder at any time—if a policeman did he should be out of the force—but this one had implications far beyond the ordinary . . .

"How?" barked the superintendent.

"Probably manual strangulation, Dr. Dabbe thinks." Of all lethal weapons two human hands left almost the least trace of all.

"When?"

"Dr. Dabbe said it was too soon for him to say." Sloan granted that a damp ditch wasn't the easiest setting in which a consultant pathologist could exercise his professional judgement and was personally prepared to await a calculated answer to that question.

The superintendent drummed his fingers on his desk. "If she's from Braffle Episcopi," he growled, "why does her body turn up beside the main road between Calleford and Berebury?"

It was Inspector Harpe who had supplied Sloan with the answer to that question. Happy Harry and the men of Traffic Division had at once sped out to the spot where the murder victim had been found, in an endeavour both to keep the traffic moving and to let those with duties at the scene have somewhere to park their vehicles. Police photographers—let alone forensic pathologists—did not take kindly to using shanks' pony.

Sloan drew breath and tried to convey the information as cogently as he could to his superior officer. He hadn't really got time for this sort of dialogue. "There's a really long natural curve on the road there, sir, which has got a good enough run into it at each end for someone parked where it bends most of all to have time to punt a body into the ditch with the driver's own car giving the maximum cover. If the road was clear both ways before you started you'd have time."

Leeyes grunted.

"There's even a bit of a lay-by there . . ."

"And had she been having a bit of a lay-by, too?" enquired Leeyes sardonically. "Or hasn't the doctor got round to that yet?"

"Dr. Dabbe has promised us a full report as soon as possible," responded Sloan with a certain reserve. One thing he could be sure about was that the doctor's observations, when they did come, would be couched in medical Latin and not in either slang or euphemism.

"So," deduced Leeyes, "it's either a local man or someone with a good eye for the country."

"It looks very much like it, sir." Sloan had hardly had time to think that through properly yet either. It was much too soon for detailed conclusions of any sort.

"Why not go into a wood and put the body somewhere where it isn't likely to be found so soon?" demanded Leeyes. "Instead of just leaving it in a ditch . . ."

"Everyone knows that tyres leave tracks," responded Sloan with only half his mind. "They learn it at play school. Perhaps whoever killed her wasn't strong enough to carry her far. Perhaps her disappearance would amount to much the same thing as her murder." He would be going over to Braffle Episcopi just as soon as he could.

The superintendent drummed his fingers on the top of his desk. "I'm afraid there's something going on that we don't know about."

"Several things," interjected Sloan swiftly.

"What's that? Oh yes, of course," grunted Leeyes. "Naturally. Unless, of course, this was just an ordinary pick-up that went wrong."

"Bit of a coincidence if it was, sir," said Sloan. "Besides, it would be too much to hope for." On second thoughts he wasn't quite sure that he really meant that exactly.

It was just that that sort of coincidence—if such it were—would lift some of the burden of regret and responsibility from police shoulders—not all of it, of course—but life—alas—wasn't like that.

Nor was death.

Superintendent Leeyes brought his eyebrows together in a fierce glare. "Puts a new light on the Carline case if it isn't a coincidence, doesn't it, Sloan?" he said to his subordinate across the desk.

"I'm afraid so, sir."

"Things not being quite what they seemed," said Leeyes heavily.

Sloan had hardly begun to consider—he hadn't had time to think about—the new vistas opened up by the murder of the Allsworthys' French *au pair* girl as they related to the case of the Crown versus Lucy Mirabel Durmast. At sight they seemed almost limitless.

"Now that we know who the victim is," went on Leeyes, "I can confirm for what it is worth that she had been reported missing to the Calleford Police." The superintendent waved a flimsy piece of paper at Sloan. "By the Allsworthys at Braffle Episcopi, late last night when their French *au pair* girl, Hortense Fablon, didn't come home on the last bus or telephone to say what had happened to her."

"I'll be getting over there just as soon as I leave here, sir," Sloan responded to the sentiment rather than the song, "and then I've got to meet Dr. Dabbe at the mortuary."

"Keep me in the picture." The superintendent nodded jerkily. "I can only call this a most unexpected development."

Detective Constable Crosby had described it as a proper turn-up for the book, but that had been in private.

"But why Hortense?" cried Mrs. Allsworthy.

"We don't know yet, madam."

The Cecelia Allsworthy to whom Detective Inspector Sloan was speaking was neither the serene wife of the lord of the manor nor an artist struggling for mastery over her chosen medium. She was a very deeply upset young woman trying without success to control her tears.

"And who would want to kill Hortense anyway?" she asked for the hundredth time.

"We don't know, madam," said Sloan seriously, "but someone did and we shall do our best to find out who it was."

"There is no possibility, then, of her death being an accident?" asked John Allsworthy. He was sitting by his wife's side, one arm round her shoulders.

"None," said Sloan shortly. He hadn't had Dr. Dabbe's full report yet but with a few well-chosen observations the pathologist had excluded suicide, accident and natural causes.

Which left only murder.

"Poor, poor Hortense," said Cecelia. "She was only having an evening out with a friend."

John Allsworthy expanded on this for the policemen's benefit. "Hortense always went into Calleford on Thursday evenings . . ."

Sloan got out his notebook with relief. It was facts that caught murderers in the long run. "How?"

"The six o'clock bus from Braffle Episcopi." Cecelia's husband had a pleasant, rather deep voice. "Cecelia and I coped with the twins ourselves and then had supper together." He tightened his grip on his wife's arm. "It's something I rather look forward to."

"Quite so." Detective Inspector Sloan read the message that John Allsworthy was trying to convey loud and clear.

"Hortense had something to eat before she left," put in Cecelia anxiously. "She didn't go out hungry or anything."

Sloan nodded. But, like the sun-tanned invalid whose last holiday had done him good before he died, it hadn't saved her.

"I mean," hastened on Cecelia Allsworthy, "she didn't need to go out with anyone for a meal," her voice fell away "or anything . . ."

"I understand, madam," he cleared his throat. "What did she go into Calleford for?"

"The Film Society," said Cecelia Allsworthy. "They have showings of foreign films there, and whenever there was a French one on she and her friend Clémence would go. They're fellow exiles."

"I see."

"They were both thoroughly homesick," said Cecelia. "Clémence is with some people who live in Luston and she and Hortense met up as often as they could at the Film Society."

"And then?" enquired Sloan.

"They caught their respective buses home. The last ones, of course."

"The last bus for Luston must leave before the last one this way," said Sloan, "because of its being so much further away."

"That's right," agreed Cecelia. "Clémence always has a scramble to catch it and Hortense a bit of a wait for hers."

"So," said Sloan, "if Clémence caught the Luston bus all right there should have been no possibility of Hortense having missed hers."

"No, none, Inspector. That's what worried us from the beginning."

"And did—er—Clémence catch her bus?" enquired Sloan.

"Oh yes." Mrs. Allsworthy nodded vigorously. "The first thing we did when Hortense didn't come in off the last bus was to telephone the people Clémence is staying with."

"And?"

"Clémence had got back there without any problems at her usual time." Now that Cecelia had something definite to say, her voice steadied. "Clémence said she'd left Hortense at the bus station in the usual way."

"And then?" asked Sloan.

John Allsworthy stirred and took up the tale. "We waited a little while in case she telephoned or came in. At first we thought she might have got a lift from someone coming this way or something."

Sloan nodded. "And after that?"

"I got the car out and went into Calleford in case she was still hanging about looking for a taxi."

"We were a bit worried in case she'd started to walk and been picked up." Cecelia turned a distraught face towards the detective inspector and said tremulously, "That's what must have happened, isn't it?"

"It's too soon to say," said Sloan. He turned back to John Allsworthy. "What did you do after that, sir?"

"I came back home," he said, "and telephoned the police to report her missing."

"Did you see or talk to anyone while you were out?"

He shook his head. "Not a soul."

"When did you get back?"

John Allsworthy shot a quick glance at his wife. "I'm not sure. I must have been gone well over an hour, mustn't I?"

"Nearly two, darling," said Cecelia Allsworthy in a strained voice. "It seemed ages, I know. I couldn't sleep."

"And you telephoned the police, sir, as soon as you got back?"

He ran a hand through his hair. "We stood in the kitchen for a minute or two talking about what to do next."

"I had some coffee on the stove," said Cecelia, a quaver in her voice, "for three."

The telephone call to the Calleford Police was a fixed point in Detective Inspector Sloan's timetable of the murder of Hortense Fablon. "I'm afraid I shall have to ask you to identify her officially —in the absence of her parents."

Allsworthy squared his shoulders. "Of course, Inspector."

"There's one other thing, sir."

"What's that?"

"Might we see your car, please?"

"Mine?" John Allsworthy looked startled and then collected himself. "Why, yes, of course."

"John's car?" Cecelia Allsworthy stared. "What do you want to look at John's car for?" She looked from one policeman to the other. "My God, Inspector, you don't think . . ."

"Think what?" asked Sloan mildly.

There was no answer. A sobbing Cecelia Allsworthy had buried her head in her husband's jacket.

"Welcome, gentlemen," said Dr. Dabbe hospitably, waving an arm round the post-mortem laboratory. "Do come in. Standing room only though, I'm afraid."

Detective Inspector Sloan edged his way into the crowded mortuary, followed by Detective Constable Crosby. He nodded to the Scenes of Crime Officer and a new young fingerprint man as he did so. The police photographers, Williams and his assistant, Dyson, were old colleagues and greeted him as he advanced.

"We've done all the outdoor stuff, Inspector," said Williams.

"We've been on a course," said Dyson, patting a new and different camera with something like affection. "Ever so clever we are now with our pictures."

"Video," explained Williams. "All the rage at post-mortems these days."

"The wonders of modern science," said Sloan suitably impressed, "will never cease."

"Worth a bit on the Saturday night market, this sort of video," said Dyson.

Crosby was quite scornful. "Dull stuff compared with what you can hire," he said.

"We'll have to make sure you don't flog 'em afterwards," said Sloan genially, "even if it is pretty tame by Crosby's standards."

"Crown copyright," said Williams without heat, "more's the pity."

"Doesn't save any paperwork," said Dr. Dabbe. "That's one thing you can all be quite sure about. Burns, my gown please . . ."

The pathologist's assistant, a perennially silent man, moved forward at once and tied the strings of the doctor's green operating gown behind him.

"Burns," continued Dr. Dabbe, "these officers are particularly interested in the subject's clothes."

"Nothing's been touched, Doctor. Everything's still in the bag."

As Sloan watched, the pathologist's assistant slide a large sealed black plastic bag onto the mortuary equivalent of an operating theatre table he wished that the same could be said for the murderer of Hortense Fablon.

And of Kenneth Carline?

If they were one and the same, then there was one person who hadn't—who couldn't have—killed the French girl because she was safe and sound in H. M. Prison Cottingham Grange. That had been checked. An alert Governor had treated their query very seriously indeed but had come back to them with great celerity to say that a roll call had accounted for everyone including Durmast, Lucy Mirabel.

"The subject," intoned Burns lugubriously, "has been formally identified by John Allsworthy, Esquire, of the Manor House, Braffle Episcopi, as that of Hortense Marie Fablon of St. Amand-sur-Nesque, Département Congre in Provence, France."

Allsworthy hadn't enjoyed doing it.

Detective Inspector Sloan knew that. He had stayed with Allsworthy while he did so for reasons of his own. And had noted how shaken the man had been. But not as disturbed as he had been by the discovery by the two detectives of Hortense Fablon's scarf in his car. Shocked to his wattles he had been by that and Sloan and Crosby had been there to witness his discomfiture and to listen to his stammered insistence that it must have been there for days.

" 'Mademoiselle from Armentières,' " hummed Dr. Dabbe irreverently, " 'hasn't been kissed for forty years.' "

"Parlez-vous," said Williams entering into the spirit of things.

"It's a scarf we're looking for," said Sloan.

"No scarf," said Burns briefly.

"Jacket, skirt and blouse," agreed the pathologist, "but no scarf."

"Ah."

"It wasn't lying in the field or anything," said the Scenes of Crime Officer. "The boys did a quick search before we left and they would have noticed a scarf. They're going over it again, of course," he added hastily, "in case they've missed anything."

"And it wasn't used to throttle her," said Dr. Dabbe. "There's no sign of a ligature of any sort having been used. It's not that sort of engorgement . . ."

Sloan noticed Detective Constable Crosby inch his way a little farther away from the centre of the scene. Crosby didn't like it when the pathologist used the sort of words that conjured up the thought of greater horror to come. Sloan was prepared to bet that the constable would have his back to the wall of the post-mortem theatre—literally—in no time at all.

And his eyes closed soon after.

"The rest of the clothing does not appear to have been disturbed," said Dr. Dabbe.

"It might have been someone she knew and trusted," said Sloan reluctantly.

"We'll do fingernail scrapings," said the pathologist, "but it doesn't look to me as she put up much of a fight."

"Taken by surprise," said Sloan sadly. "That's what it looks like to me."

"I daresay," said Dr. Dabbe. "Keep an eye on her clothes, all the same, Burns. I can't see any tears or pulled threads, but you never know. We don't want the forensic science lads getting above themselves, do we?"

"There's mud on them, of course," said the Scenes of Crime man. "I've got some from the site, too, to compare it with."

"Good," said Sloan absently. "What are the shoes like?"

"Clean," said Burns.

It was all adding up, noted Sloan, as the pathologist commenced his external examination of the body proper, to Hortense Fablon having accepted a lift from someone she knew—not even of her having set off to walk anywhere. Then having been suddenly attacked and her body driven to this choice spot on the Berebury-to-Calleford road that could only have been known to someone who knew the area well.

And since the number of Englishmen whom she knew was necessarily limited . . .

"I'm having the larynx X-rayed before I go any further," announced Dr. Dabbe suddenly. "That'll tell us if there are fractures of the hyoid bone and thyroid cartilages. I'm afraid there will be some delay while we get a radiographer over . . ."

There was a general slackening of tension in the post-mortem room while the obedient Burns went off to telephone.

"Got a motive yet, Sloan?" asked Dr. Dabbe informally.

"I'm beginning," said Sloan, "to be very much afraid that it might have been because of something that she knew."

The pathologist quoted A. H. Clough, a poet popular with the medical profession for quite the wrong reasons, with relish:

> "Swans sing before they die: t'were no bad thing,
> Some men should die before they sing."

"But," said Sloan, "I'm blessed if I know what Hortense Fablon knew or can have known that was a danger to anyone." He frowned. "It must be tied in in some way with the Carline murder but don't ask me how . . ."

"I heard about that from young Dr. Bressingham over at Calleford," said Dabbe. "He's just settling in."

"The Durmasts and the Allsworthys are practically next-door neighbours at Braffle Episcopi," said Sloan. "And they are friends too."

"There's more than one way of killing a canary," said the pathologist, adding thoughtfully, "or two canaries."

"It can't be coincidence," said Sloan.

"Poisoning, wasn't it?"

"Hyoscine."

"A woman's weapon, poison." Someone else had said that too. Before Dr. Dabbe.

"A lethal dose of hyoscine in the chili con carne. At least," Sloan corrected himself, "a lethal dose of hyoscine in the deceased." He mustn't forget that he was somewhere where accuracy counted above almost everything else. "We presumed it was in the chili con carne."

"Ah."

"She served it with something called samphire." Sloan tried to remember who it was who had said "Accuracy is not a virtue, it is a duty."

"Salicornia," said Dr. Dabbe. "There'll be plenty of that on the shore their way."

"And if Lucy Durmast didn't kill Kenneth Carline," said Sloan, "I don't know who did."

The pathologist pointed to the supine body of Hortense Fablon. "That was man's work, Sloan, unless I'm very much mistaken."

"Lucy Durmast had everything," said Sloan, following an earlier train of thought. "Means, motive, opportunity."

"Doesn't mean, old chap, that someone else hadn't as well . . ." The pathologist looked up as a helmeted police dispatch rider appeared at the mortuary door. "Yes?"

"I'm looking for Detective Constable Crosby, sir."

The pathologist waved an arm. "Over there."

The dispatch rider handed an envelope to Crosby.

Detective Inspector Sloan watched the transaction with mingled irritation and curiosity.

"I told them to send it on," said Crosby in a lordly way.

"Send what?" asked Sloan.

"That report we were waiting for," said the constable.

Sloan frowned, unable to recollect any missing report.

"You know, sir," said Crosby. "On the Rugby match that Kenneth Durmast got knocked about in."

Sloan let out a sigh of pure exasperation.

"You did ask for it this morning," said Crosby in injured tones.

"All right," said Sloan resignedly. This morning seemed aeons away. This morning they hadn't known about the murder of Hortense Fablon. "Let me have a look at it."

The reportage was enthusiastic, if amateur. The column was headed "Calleford 11, Luston 18":

A superb second half display of fine tackling inspired Luston to victory over their old adversaries, Calleford. It was Luston's most impressive performance of the season. In spite of two late tries Calleford never looked like winning. Luston took the lead early with a penalty from Wilkins followed by a successful drop kick.

Calleford's spirited attempts to hit back particularly by Carline, were tempered by dedicated tackling on the part of Hirst and by midway through the second half Carline was practically a marked man. Carline came out of a loose scrum bloodied but unbowed but even so Hirst intercepted his best pass and sprinted 50 yards for a try converted by Wilkins; clinching victory.

Play up, play up, play the game, thought Sloan sourly to himself, except that Hirst didn't seem to have played it very fairly. Rugby was Verdun all over again. He handed the report back to Crosby. "I don't think we ought to change course because of this . . ."

As he was later to be the first to admit, he had seldom been more wrong.

SIXTEEN

Cataplasma—The poultices

One of the favourite quotations of Detective Inspector Sloan's mother was "Without haste, without rest" and Sloan was bound to admit that nothing fitted the ideal pace for a murder investigation better than this. It might have been medieval moralists who equated haste with evil but it went for today, too, as far as he, Sloan, was concerned. Morning had stretched into afternoon and late afternoon had merged imperceptibly into early evening without haste but without rest either.

By then he had been barely conscious of time. His evening meal of the day before seemed in retrospect to have been unconscionably leisured in comparison with the few snatched bites of today. Both he and Crosby had eaten on the hoof, so to speak, while the wheels of a full-scale murder enquiry had been set in motion. A tearful Clémence had been interviewed in Luston by an officer proficient not only in French but in the patois of Clémence's native département.

The girls had been to see a film called *Le Proie* and had parted as usual at the bus station. Hortense had not mentioned having a *rendez-vous clandestin* to her friend Clémence, but that didn't prove anything, did it? Absence of evidence, the interrogating officer had remarked in his report, not being the same thing at all as evidence of absence, adding by way of gilding the French lily, *"Après moi le déluge."*

"Queen Anne's dead," Sloan had retorted pretty speedily to that.

The ticket inspector at the Calleford bus station hadn't noticed a girl answering to Hortense's description waiting for the last bus to Marby juxta Mare, but that was just about the time he had his break from duty. Pressed, he admitted that a car could easily have pulled into and out of the bus station without his having heard it.

He doubted if he would have recognised it if he had seen it, cars being all alike these days. The night cleaner at the bus station knew nothing about cars except that she was never going to be able to afford one. And that they weren't good news for bus companies.

There were two more people, though, whom Detective Inspector Sloan was determined to interview before the day was out and before he went back to have another session with John Allsworthy at Braffle Episcopi. One was Ronald Bolsover. Sloan and Crosby tracked him down to his home on the outskirts of Calleford. He was in his hot-house, attending to the plants when they arrived. The deputy chairman of Durmast's saw them coming up the path and beckoned them in that way.

"Cecelia Allsworthy telephoned me," he said soberly. "Poor child."

"Did you know her?" asked Sloan.

"I suppose, Inspector," said Bolsover, "it would be more correct to say that I knew of her rather than that I actually knew her."

"Hot in here, isn't it?" remarked Crosby, running a finger along inside his collar.

"I knew that she suffered from homesickness because Cecelia used to say," carried on the deputy chairman, "that she was going to send her—Hortense was her name, wasn't it?—was going to send her over to sit in my greenhouse to remind her of home."

"I can see why," said Sloan.

"The bougainvillae might have helped," said Bolsover.

"You've got some fine plants here," said Sloan, looking round with a connoisseur's eye.

"And the hibiscus." Bolsover continued with his theme. "That's common enough where she comes from."

"So's that." Sloan pointed to a healthy-looking oleander. "I don't know its neighbour though."

"West Indian Jasmine," said Bolsover with pardonable pride. He moved down the hot-house. "What do you think of this, Inspector?"

"It's erythrina, isn't it?"

"That's right." Bolsover nodded. "The coral tree. Are you interested in semi-tropical stuff, Inspector?"

"Roses, mostly," replied Sloan briefly. This was an official visit.

"What about this then?" Bolsover halted in front of a Dionaea.

"Venus fly trap," said Sloan unhesitatingly. For some obscure reason that he hadn't time to explore, this brought him back to his duties as an investigating officer. "I shall need to know where everyone was last night."

"I quite understand." Bolsover nodded. "Actually I was at home all yesterday evening, Inspector. I'd just bought that new plant over there and I was potting it up. Bauhinia. I've never grown it before."

"And your wife?" asked Sloan. Hot-houses were all right for some, but they cost money keeping at the right temperature.

"In London. She's gone up for a two-day china and porcelain sale. She collects Bow, you know. She stayed overnight."

"I see, sir." Out of the corner of his eye Sloan saw Crosby writing that down.

"I worked late, as she wasn't going to be here, and then I came home and did the watering." Bolsover smiled. "At least Bow china doesn't need much attention. Then I got myself some supper and eventually went to bed."

Sloan nodded as Crosby made his notes. From where he stood— literally—he could see that there would be nothing to be gained by involving the Bolsovers' neighbours in the confirmation of this. The house was sufficiently detached for an unlit car to slip in and out unseen. But as to why the deputy chairman of Durmast's should want to kill a French *au pair* girl, Sloan could think of no reason at all and soon set about taking his leave.

"Inspector"—Bolsover became suddenly diffident—"tell me, does the killing of this French lass have any bearing at all on the charge against Lucy Durmast?"

"Does it let her out, you mean?" Detective Constable Crosby did a quick literal translation of Ronald Bolsover's careful prose for everyone's benefit.

"Too soon to say," responded Sloan repressively. Crosby wasn't there to rephrase the remarks of the person being interviewed. He would have to speak to him about that. "It might have everything to do with it. On the other hand it might have nothing at all . . ."

Crosby was quite undeterred. "Like the man who wanted a one-armed lawyer so that he couldn't say 'on the other hand.' "

"Crosby!"

"Sorry, sir."

Bolsover said quietly, "If you do have any news on that front, Inspector, it would be a help. I feel I have a heavy responsibility to

Bill Durmast even though I respect Lucy's motives in keeping him out of the picture." He essayed a faint smile. "If you're in a situation where client variation orders are delivered with a shrunken head to go with them, you don't want trouble at home as well."

"Quite so," said Sloan noncommittally, turning to go.

"What's that one called?" asked Crosby, pointing to a plant as he put his notebook away.

"Haemanthus," answered Ronald Bolsover.

"Blood lily," said Sloan. "Come along, Crosby . . ."

Once upon a time—more especially, that is, in the time when she had been a free woman—Lucy Durmast had read a marvellous book about solitary confinement. It had been written by a man who had experienced it in Fresnes prison in France during the last war and who therefore could be presumed to have known his subject. One of the observations he had made about his incarceration Lucy had at the time read with a certain amount of disbelief.

This was how he had come to dislike being interrupted.

Far from welcoming the distraction—any distraction—he had, after a time, come to resent it, preferring instead to continue with whatever train of thought he had embarked upon without interruption. Lucy wasn't in solitary confinement in H. M. Prison Cottingham Grange—not in any physical sense, that is—but she, too, was coming to see intrusions from the world outside her cell as disturbances.

Now for the first time she fully understood that writer. For one fragile moment as well she had also come near to believing that she could begin at last to understand something—but only something —of the way of life of a contemplative religious, but she had dismissed the notion as laughable as quickly as it had come to her. Actually there wasn't much that was laughable in Cottingham Grange—prisons weren't strong on humour. The risible is always a challenge to authority—Lucy knew that from her own schooldays—and the facetious simply did not arise.

Nevertheless she had found it interesting to see where undiverted trains of thought led. And had appreciated how a nun concentrating exclusively on a particular subject could reach greater heights of spirituality than someone interrupted by the mundane—the Mary and Martha conflict. The distractions of prison life were pitifully few and far between—even for the Marthas of this world. Meals, exercise, roll-call, work in the kitchens, constituted the daily round—this last much prized in prison, which, thought Lucy astringently, was rather illogical considering that there were those in the outside world who saw such work in the kitchen at home as prison. As for the phrase "Women's Lib," it had connotations of irony in H. M. Cottingham Grange that verged on the sublime.

What was in Lucy's mind at the moment and was engaging her full attention was the search for a word.

The longest one that she knew—antidisestablishmentarianism— had gone roiling about in her mind long after the chaplain's visit while she had sought another one: the word which all the vowels in the English language appeared in their right alphabetical order. She had known it well enough in the second form at school. Her cell-mates would have been surprised if they had known what it was she was cudgelling her brains trying to remember but they wouldn't have objected. Their attitude to her silence had interested Lucy by its very practicality.

"Quite right, dear," the oldest one had said. "Say nothing. It's the only thing they can't hold against you."

"Least said, soonest mended's what I always say," nodded another. "Especially in Court."

"Never had no time for canaries myself," said a self-possessed girl called Rita. "You keep quiet if you want to. No skin off our noses, is it?"

At least, thought Lucy silently, she had one advantage over that prisoner of the Germans in the book. No one was going to drag her from her cell and say—and, alas, mean—"We have ways of making you talk."

In England you went to prison as punishment, not *for* punishment. There was both a distinction and a difference. There was one thing, though, that did belong entirely to the prison ambience and of which Lucy was very aware. In a prison cell you were no longer mistress of your own front door. There was, she realised now, more than one way of looking at a key. It both opened a door and kept it locked. The difference there lay in whose hand it was held. Rather like the distinction between a master key and a skeleton one. It was the same key opening the same door but for different reasons and in different hands.

She was no longer mistress of her own front door.

She had no power to exclude the world.

When the door of her room was unceremoniously opened and she was told that Detective Inspector Sloan of the Berebury Criminal Investigation Department wanted to see her, she rose without demur. Detective Inspector Porritt had been persistent, polite and very much to the point and she had no cause to believe that Detective Inspector Sloan wouldn't be as well. After all, she wasn't an anchorite—or was it an eremite?—with her thoughts as her raison d'être. "I think, therefore I am . . ." No, that was something else. Or was it?

Detective Inspector Sloan and Detective Constable Crosby interviewed Lucy in one of the visiting rooms at the prison. Like Detective Inspector Porritt, Sloan was persistent, polite and pertinent but he was now a man with extra purpose.

"I must ask for your full cooperation," he said. "Matters have taken a very tragic turn."

She looked at him without comment, determined now not to be tricked into speech.

"There are several things I need to know, miss," he said earnestly, "and rather quickly."

She remained gravely attentive.

"Perhaps," he said, "you would just give me a sign that you agree or disagree with what I am saying."

She stiffened. This was a new ploy and she knew where it would lead to. The unguarded nod, the deliberate misunderstanding on the part of the interrogator causing inadvertent speech . . .

When his question came it merely puzzled her.

As far as she knew Kenneth Carline hadn't known Hortense Fablon, but she didn't say so. She remained rigid in her chair, her arms folded in her lap throughout the Detective Inspector's visit. At one point she detached her mind from them altogether and went back to considering which word in the English language it was that had all the vowels in it in the right alphabetical order . . .

"You see, miss," a voice was saying as if from afar, "this is a very serious business indeed. Something has happened which may or may not have repercussions on the case against you. I can't say for sure, of course."

She was aware of his persuasiveness. From where she sat the policemen appeared to be full of honest endeavour, but appearances were deceptive. There was no one better placed than Lucy herself to know this . . .

"Events," he said, "have taken a very unhappy turn indeed."

A word in the English language which used all five vowels in alphabetical order . . .

"I'm very much afraid that someone else has been killed," the policeman said.

Five vowels, thought Lucy desperately.

"Someone you know, Miss Durmast."

Fear clutched at her heart. They were wrong, those clinicians who insisted that that organ should be thought of as a pump. She distinctly felt her heart contract as he spoke. Pumps didn't change gear when alarmed. Her eyes asked the question that her tongue could not. Literally could not, now. It clove to her palate, too dry to move.

"Someone from Braffle Episcopi," said Sloan.

Five vowels in the right order.

The answer suddenly welled up from her memory with the same apparent illogicality as a fact summoned up by computer from the depths of an impersonal machine. She suddenly thought how equally unlikely both storage and retrieval systems looked—brain and software. Human and mechanical. There wasn't much to choose between them as improbable sources of recorded information.

Five vowels in the right order occurred in the word "facetious."

She had to make herself turn her head and focus on what Detective Inspector Sloan was saying.

"Hortense Fablon, Mrs. Allsworthy's *au pair*, was killed last night."

There was, the policemen discovered, yet another variation on human communication. It fell awkwardly between the verbal and the non-verbal but whose meaning was as clear as any in either category.

Lucy Durmast burst into tears.

"Where to?" asked Crosby, as the gates of H. M. Prison Cottingham Grange clanged behind them and they were back in the outside uncloistered world.

"Headquarters," said Detective Inspector Sloan, "to collect a warrant."

"Right, sir."

"Then out to Braffle Episcopi again."

Crosby put his foot down on the accelerator.

"There's no hurry," said Sloan. "Allsworthy won't run away. That sort doesn't. He'll face the music, all right. And his wife'll stand by him. That sort always does. Besides, I want to think . . ."

He shut his eyes.

That wasn't so much as an aid to thought as an attempt as determined as that of Lucy Durmast's to exclude the world. If he kept them open he would have to devote the journey to wishing he had led a better life and there wasn't time for that now. With Crosby at the wheel, self-preservation demanded muscles braced for whatever was to come. He had duties that shouldn't be subsumed by such mental and physical distraction . . .

He would read Dr. Dabbe's report, of course, before he went out to Braffle Episcopi.

He'd give John Allsworthy every chance to explain why he had been so long in Calleford looking for Hortense Fablon.

And so late in reporting her missing to the police.

And being so put out by the finding of her scarf in his car.

For all he knew, *droit de seigneur* was something the French girl understood very well. Perhaps Dr. Dabbe would be able to give him the answer to that too. The pathologist's phraseology would be different but his meaning undeniably clear.

He opened his eyes briefly and shut them again.

The words *droit de seigneur* came from the French. Hortense would have known what they mean all right. For all he knew there was a lord of the manor at St. Amand-sur-Nesque who, like John Allsworthy, owned the best house and most of the land and who was accustomed to having his way with young girls working in the house . . .

He opened his eyes again and this time he kept them open. "You might remember, Crosby, that overtaking leads to undertaking."

"Well?" barked Leeyes as they walked into his office at Berebury Police Station.

"No joy from Lucy Durmast, sir."

"She wouldn't tell you anything about this fellow Allsworthy and the French girl then?"

"She wouldn't tell me anything full stop, sir," said Sloan.

"Not even," said Leeyes richly, "that they were just good friends?"

"She cried," reported Sloan in a constrained way, "but she didn't say anything."

Leeyes was professionally proof against tears. He was strong on circumstantial evidence though. "This scarf, Sloan . . ."

"Hortense Fablon's," said Sloan.

"In his car?"

"Indubitably," affirmed Sloan. "The wife said the French girl had missed it the day before."

"Wives," said Leeyes darkly, "will say anything."

"Yes, sir. He had given the girl a lift a few days earlier into Edsway. There's a chemist's there."

"Two crimes of passion in one village," mused Leeyes, "seem a bit much, all the same . . ." He was interrupted by the sudden shrill of the telephone on his desk. "Yes?" he said abruptly into the receiver. "I thought I said I wasn't to be disturbed. What's that?" His voice rose. "What did you say? Say it again!" he commanded, and then "Is he sure? What was he doing? Where? When?" There was a pause, then the Superintendent slammed the receiver down. "That was a report of a message from that man Bolsover from Calleford."

"Yes?"

"He just went out to a Chinese takeaway . . ."

"And?"

"He's quite sure he saw Prince Aturu in the High Street there a few minutes ago."

SEVENTEEN

Spiritus—Spirits

When he reviewed the case of Regina versus Lucy Mirabel Durmast afterwards, Detective Inspector Sloan was inclined to indicate among the sympathetic privacy of his peers that the search for Prince Aturu of Dlasa was almost the most anxiety-provoking part of the whole affair.

Looking for a man for whom no really accurate description had been available was bad enough: circumventing a humourous attempt to give the exercise the code name "Liquorice Allsorts" had been blood-chilling in its public relations implications. Before Superintendent Leeyes got to hear about it, Sloan settled with a neat sense of history for "Operation Black Prince" instead.

A hastily summoned Dr. Adam Chelde came up with some academic words about Prince Aturu such as "dolicocephalic" which were no doubt accurate but scarcely helpful.

"What's that?" was Detective Constable Crosby's immediate reaction. "Never heard of it."

Dr. Chelde came from a background where it was perfectly proper to proclaim one's ignorance. "Not your field, of course, Officer," he said generously. "It means long-headed."

Ronald Bolsover, when consulted, had been vaguer. "Tall and black. Looked as if he would have made an athlete, I shouldn't wonder. Very African, anyway."

Since the number of races in Africa was legion, this was not really very constructive.

James Jeavington, the civil servant at the Ministry for Overseas Development, had spoken about the man's hair. "Bound to have been crinkly," he said. "All Dlasians have short crinkly hair."

Asked about the shape of Dlasian heads, he was more graphic

than the Dean of Cremond had been. "Pear-drop," he said phytomorphologically.

Kenneth Durmast's three flat-mates had been the least observant of all.

"Marvellous teeth," said Alan Marshall who had suffered young at the dentist's hands.

"A rich, plummy sort of voice," said Colin Jervis, who was the one who worked in the bank. Sloan put the association between money and intonation (if there was one) to the back of his mind for future examination.

Gerry Porteous had been the most perceptive. "He sort of walked tall, if you know what I mean, Inspector. Like a king's son should."

A general alert had accordingly gone out to all police divisions in Calleshire to seek and detain anyone answering to the composite description of Prince Aturu. The trawl netted a veritable anthropologist's dream.

Two West Indians who worked in Calleford Hospital were positively affronted at being mistaken for Dlasian, a country for which they had no reverence at all. A merchant seaman from Mhlamaland, whose people had been hereditary enemies of the Dlasians for generations, became very combative and showed every sign of becoming a hereditary enemy of the Calleshire County Constabulary as well.

A highly civilised merchant from Bengal with commercial business to execute in Luston, asked by a police sergeant where he was going, raised his hat and replied, "Almstone, sir," adding with Olde Worlde courtesy to the officer, "and you?"

A newly arrived visiting professor of physics from Alabama, come to take up the Ornum Fellowships at the University of Calleshire, rather sadly recast his first letter home that evening, while the deepest forebodings of a South American tourist were confirmed by a simple enquiry about where he had come from made by a police constable in Berebury.

The greatest confusion of all arose during an interview with a strapping youth of the darkest of skins, seen running towards Calleford railway station. Asked from whence he had come, he said in the broadest of accents, "Lancashire." Asked where he had been born, he gave the same reply. Asked his nationality he said "British." He demanded rather pugnaciously to see the enquiring officer's credentials and started to talk about writs of habeas corpus, both of which the policeman concerned treated as evidence of long residence in the United Kingdom.

"British is best," the young man grinned, offering to race the policeman to the railway station, "but Black British is better."

When the nature of the enquiry was explained to him, he remarked ironically, "You have got trouble at t'mill, haven't you, man?" and sped on his way.

Detective Inspector Sloan, whose personal view was that what really divided mankind irrespective of everything else was a preference for thick or thin gravy, eviscerated all the reports with great speed and established one essential fact.

Of Prince Aturu of Dlasa there was not a single sign anywhere in the county of Calleshire.

William Shakespeare, decided Detective Inspector Sloan, had been quite wrong about sleep knitting up the ravelled sleeve of care. The Bard might, of course, have been talking about real sleep. Fitful dozes through the night had done nothing for Sloan.

Late late night thoughts had been succeeded by early early thoughts without a conscious distinction between the two and morning had broken without enlightenment.

Whoever it had been, he thought sourly, as he plastered his face with shaving cream, who had written about bright new day had never been faced with untangling three mysteries that might or might not have been connected but that were certainly plaited together: the murder of Kenneth Carline, the disruption of the tunnel-opening ceremony by anti-nuclear protesters, and the unlawful killing of Hortense Fablon.

It was an exceedingly unholy trinity.

The three balls of the Medici didn't have anything on it.

Perm any two, as the punters said.

Or three.

Or none.

The smell of bacon being fried drifted upstairs but did not cheer him.

Even the classic question in detection of "Who benefits?" didn't help.

Answer came there none to that.

A diligent Inspector Porritt had researched Kenneth Carline's background to establish beyond any doubt that no one benefited financially by his death.

It was highly unlikely that anyone gained from Hortense Fablon's death either.

But why two murders?

Unbidden, as philosophers have found is the way while shaving, Lady Bracknell's immortal lines came into his mind. "To lose one parent, Mr. Worthing, may be regarded as a misfortune; to lose both looks like carelessness."

He frowned. He'd had that thought before recently but in a different connection.

The aroma of percolating coffee pursued the smell of fried bacon up the stairs while he tried to pin down in his mind when and why he'd thought it before.

Had it been yesterday or was it the day before when something else had struck him briefly in the same way?

He stared unseeingly into the mirror while he searched his memory. It had been something to do with something about Kenneth Durmast and Cecelia Allsworthy had said it . . . that much he did remember.

"Breakfast," called out Margaret Sloan.

He didn't hear her.

It had come back to him what it was that Cecelia Allsworthy had said that had provoked the quotation the first time.

Had he been a fisherman, Sloan would have placed the moment as that when the float on the surface of the water first twitched.

As any really experienced angler could have told him he was still a long way from having his fish caught, landed and safely in the keep net.

Detective Constable Crosby was waiting for him at the Police Station when Sloan arrived.

"What I'm looking for," said the Detective Inspector trenchantly, "is a hook . . ."

"Yes, sir."

"A line."

"Yes, sir."

". . . and a sinker," finished Sloan. He had walked to work and not wasted the time.

"What about a car, sir?" enquired Crosby seriously. He understood about cars.

"Not just yet, Crosby, thank you. Presently, perhaps. We've got a lot to do first. Will you ask Inspector Harpe in Traffic Division if he could spare me a minute? And get someone to bring Mrs. Melissa Wainwright in to the station." He paused. "Tell her that she will be helping the police with their enquiries. Literally." He halted. "No, that won't do. We don't want a demonstration outside the police station. Tell her we should be most obliged for her help and see if that does the trick."

"Yes, sir."

"I'll have that report about the Rugby match that you had yesterday, too."

Crosby reached for a file. "Anything else, sir?"

"A copy of the *Complete Works of William Shakespeare* would be a help. There's something in *Hamlet* I want to check."

"Yes, sir," said Crosby stolidly. "What about a warrant for John Allsworthy for murder?"

"Certainly not," said Detective Inspector Sloan briskly. "He didn't do it."

The telephone line between Berebury Police Station and the office of the Consultant Pathologist to the Berebury District General Hospital crackled as the switchboard connected Dr. Dabbe.

"That you, Sloan? Good. I've got my report all ready for you."

"Thank you, Doctor." There must be a saving grace, decided Sloan, to every murder. Like a professional conjuror, a murderer had to perform as in one of those stage acts that involved keeping an ever-increasing number of oranges in the air at the same time. Sooner or later he must make a mistake.

He—the murderer, that is—had only had the one orange to begin with: a dead engineer. To that had been added another orange —poison—and then a third: an accused girl who had stayed obdurately silent. They had to be kept in the air while the conjuror picked up another orange from his stage table. All the anomalies of a nuclear demonstration joined the other oranges in the air—an unlocked gate, an unguarded key and a mysterious telephone call said to have come from Durmast's.

And while the murderer's prestidigitatory skill was still dazzling the audience, the Dlasian oranges had to be worked in—a dissident, disappearing Prince, the new town at Mgongwala and an absent company chairman and father.

It was a dead French girl—the last orange—that had proved too much for a performer hoping that the quickness of the hand would deceive the eye, and the whole act had tumbled to the ground, coming to an ignominious end and scattering oranges everywhere . . .

"The murder of Hortense Fablon," the doctor was saying, "was —er—quite straightforward."

Detective Inspector Sloan pulled his notebook a little nearer. "No frills?"

"None," said the doctor. "Beyond any doubt death was caused by manual strangulation."

"The murderer wouldn't have had time to plan anything too elaborate," said Sloan. He knew that now.

"Quite so," rejoined the pathologist. "However, in view of what you have suggested to me in connection with an earlier death, I am having various organs analysed for traces of hyoscine."

"You never know with defence counsel," said Sloan.

"No more you do," said Dabbe warmly.

"And it can't do any harm," Sloan rationalised the matter to himself.

"Even gold has to go through the assayer's fire," said the pathologist obliquely.

"True," nodded Sloan.

"As you know, there is absolutely no clinical evidence to point to the presence of any noxious substance in the body of the deceased. Qualitative assay should confirm this."

"I'm quite sure she wasn't poisoned," said Sloan, "but it's as well to—er—leave no stone unturned." He didn't really want to know to which of the poor girl's internal organs that cliché referred, and he quickly got back to a matter that he really did need to know. "Doctor, tell me something . . ."

"*À votre service,*" said the pathologist with macabre appositeness.

"There is, of course, nothing to suggest that Hortense Fablon had been poisoned, but equally there is no doubt at all that Kenneth Durmast was."

"None," said Dr. Dabbe promptly. "My colleague Dr. Bressingham demonstrated that Durmast died from an overdose of hyoscine."

"What Inspector Porritt, my colleague, was not able to prove," said Sloan neatly, "was how the murderer got the poison into the victim."

"As I said before," repeated the doctor gravely, "there are more ways than one of killing a canary."

"What I want to know," said Sloan, "if one particular way would do the trick."

"I'm all ears," said the pathologist.

"Just so," said Sloan, embarking on a theory that might have held water for the murder of Gonzago too.

"Are you quite sure, Sloan?" growled Superintendent Leeyes.

"Not yet, sir, but I've asked Inspector Harpe to do some checking for me and we're trying to find a man called Hirst who lives in Luston."

"And who's he?" Leeyes wanted to know.

"A member of the Luston Rugby Club."

"I hope you know what you're doing, Sloan," Leeyes said irritably.

"I think," replied Detective Inspector Sloan, "that we're very near to uncovering the biggest fraud Calleshire has ever known."

Leeyes grunted. He had always insisted that the chairman of the Watch Committee deserved that particular designation. "You haven't been putting two and two together and making five, have you?"

"I've just been looking at the facts, sir," Sloan said. People used the word "kaleidoscope" so often and so loosely that its real meaning got forgotten. Sloan could still remember the wonder of first looking down the dark tube to the mirror at the other end with the fragments of coloured silver paper lying in one pattern—and giving the whole thing a jerk that produced a completely different pattern. The constituents were exactly the same—the tube was sealed, which proved it—but the total picture changed in an instant. The facts of the murder of Kenneth Carline had been there all the time. It had taken a tug at a mental kaleidoscope though to rearrange them in a formation that now made sense.

"It's evidence you'll need," said Leeyes unhelpfully.

"It was something that Crosby said about the sort of evidence we needed that helped to put me on the right lines," said Sloan.

"Crosby?" echoed Leeyes. "I don't believe it."

"He said what we needed was concrete evidence, sir, and I think that's what we'll be getting." Sloan tapped his notebook. "We're also turning up a report on a fatal road traffic accident in South Humberside something like eighteen months ago."

"Why?" grunted Leeyes.

"Kenneth Carline's predecessor died there in one." Sloan coughed. "We now have reason to believe that the death might not have been an accident." Messrs. William Durmast had lost not one young structural engineer but two. And in spite of what Lady Bracknell had said it wasn't due to carelessness but murder.

"What about this fellow that you can't find?" asked Leeyes. "Prince Monalulu."

"Aturu," Sloan corrected him. He had never met Prince Aturu but he was quite sure that the son of King Thabile III would never don feathers and go round a race course shouting "I gotta horse."

"Him," said Leeyes.

"I don't think he comes into the picture," said Sloan.

"What!"

"Oh, he was a friend of Kenneth Carline's all right and very caught up in Dlasian politics."

"And so . . ."

"And so," said Sloan, "he's gone to New York to see the United Nations."

Leeyes rolled his eyes wordlessly. "And the revenge token?"

"An artifact copied from something in the Greatorex Museum. We've checked with the curator. Apparently William Durmast presented them with the original the last time he was home."

"Do you mean to stand there and tell me that Dlasa doesn't come into this at all?"

Sloan frowned. "It's not as simple as that, sir. Perhaps I'd better explain."

"I think you had," said Superintendent Leeyes heavily. "Tell me . . ."

He sat back in his chair and listened with close attention to what Sloan said.

Presently he grunted "You're taking a warrant, aren't you, Sloan?"

"Yes, sir."

"We don't want any slip-ups at this stage."

"No, sir." Sloan was cheered by the superintendent's use of the plural of majesty. It was always a good sign.

"At home?"

"No, sir, I don't think so." Sloan coughed. "I had the scene of the crime in mind."

EIGHTEEN

Solvellae—Solution-tablets

"How could Kenneth Carline possibly have been murdered at work, Inspector?" stammered Cecelia Allsworthy.

If by any stretch of the imagination the arrest of the murderer of Kenneth Carline and Hortense Fablon had been the subject of a stage play, the time of this, the Third Act so to speak, could have been accurately described as "Later the same day." Only it seemed infinitely longer ago than this morning since Sloan had shaved, applying not only a simple blade but Occam's Razor as well.

"I just don't understand," said Cecelia. She was still shaken and unsure of herself.

The action that had begun that morning with a train of thought in front of a bathroom mirror had reached its apotheosis in the hand-cuffing of Ronald Bolsover in the offices of William Durmast in the Rushmarket in Calleford. The tragedy wasn't going to be quite over within the Aristotelian unity of one revolution of the sun, although evening had found Detective Inspector Sloan and Detective Constable Crosby sitting round the kitchen table at the Manor House at Braffle Episcopi talking to both Allsworthys.

"And why was Kenneth murdered?" Cecelia Allsworthy asked.

"It was when we started to wonder why that we found out how," said Sloan enigmatically. He was keeping one eye on the kitchen range. Cecelia Allsworthy had stood a vast saucepan of home-made soup on the hottest part and in his view wasn't giving it the attention it needed. Both policemen were hungry and Sloan didn't want the soup to boil over.

"But you've already said that everyone could see everything that Ronald Bolsover did in his office." John Allsworthy leaned forward, his eye bright with interest. "The walls are glass, aren't they?"

"That was the beauty of it," said Sloan, "and that was what gave us the clue in the end."

"What was?"

"The dumb show," said Sloan. "Like in *Hamlet.*"

Cecelia Allsworthy raised a wan face, light dawning. "Ah, I think I know now . . . the play within the play."

"Before their very eyes," said Detective Constable Crosby. "Clever, wasn't it?"

"Everyone seeing what was going on," said Sloan, "but not understanding."

"I still don't understand," said John Allsworthy firmly. "And I should like to be told. What exactly was going on?"

"Fraud, mostly," said Sloan, "and when Kenneth Carline—and his predecessor, poor chap—tumbled to it, murder as well."

"With the whole office watching?"

Sloan nodded.

"How?" demanded Allsworthy.

"When Carline got to the office on the fatal Monday morning he was in pretty bad shape—bruised and battered and so forth." Sloan began his narrative with the day of the murder.

"That was the effects of the Rugby match on the Saturday," said John Allsworthy. "Everyone knew that."

"What they didn't know," said Sloan, unperturbed, "was that a man in the opposing team had undertaken to tackle Kenneth Carline at every opportunity. He thought he was doing it for a bet."

"But he wasn't?" asked Cecelia.

"He was preparing the ground."

"What for?"

"Murder," said Sloan succinctly, "by a very clever man."

"But how?" insisted Allsworthy. "With everyone looking on."

"By the application," said Sloan steadily, "of a piece of sticking plaster behind the deceased's ear."

"That couldn't have killed," said Allsworthy.

"No," agreed Sloan, "but the hyoscine impregnated in it did. The sticking plaster had been doctored by Bolsover." It was funny how the word "doctored" had two meanings—one good and one bad. "Quite a lot of drugs can be administered transdermally."

"Through the skin," translated Detective Constable Crosby, who had had to have the concept explained to him very carefully.

"Angina pectoris," expounded Sloan, "can be treated now by

sticking a specially prepared self-adhesive patch on the skin which delivers a constant dose of glyceryl trinitrate to the patient."

"Ah . . ." Cecelia Allsworthy let out a long sigh.

"And American doctors quite often prescribe drugs in this way for travel sickness."

"Bolsover went to the States sometimes on business," said John Allsworthy.

His wife frowned. "You know, my grandmother used to talk about belladonna plasters when she was young . . ."

"Out of fashion," said Sloan, "these days but Dr. Dabbe tells me that there were occasional poisonings from them too." Actually the pathologist had used the ominous expression "recorded in the literature" and was going to send to the library.

"So," said John Allsworthy, "Bolsover stuck it on and sent Kenneth off to have lunch with Lucy?"

"That's right," said Sloan. "She was almost bound to invite him really in the circumstances and it was beautifully timed for the hyoscine to work after Carline's meal with someone who might be suspect. Bolsover took good care not to be there himself, and the fact that Lucy gave him chili con carne was just luck."

"Most Monday lunches are made-up dishes," said Cecelia sagely, "especially ones at short notice."

"The car accident," said Sloan resuming his saga, "helped to delay diagnosis and treatment, but the real object of the exercise was to make sure that Carline wasn't there for the final paperwork on the tunnel. And," he added, "to retrieve William Durmast's copy of the tunnel plans from his study."

"What has the tunnel got to do with it?" asked Cecelia.

"Everything," said Sloan. He coughed. "Excuse me, Mrs. Allsworthy, but I think that the soup might be about to boil over."

There was a concerted dive for the stove and the soup was rescued in the nick of time. John Allsworthy applied himself to cutting heroic-sized chunks of home-made bread and Cecelia came out of an old-fashioned larder with a whole ripe Stilton cheese and a bowl of apples.

"Will this do for everybody?" she asked anxiously. "I . . . we haven't felt like cooking properly since . . . since . . . since Hortense . . ." Her voice quavered and she fell silent.

"We don't really know where Hortense comes into all this, Inspector," said John Allsworthy. "If she does, that is."

"I'm afraid there's no doubt about that, sir. She comes in all right." Allsworthy had accepted with dignity the return of his car and the news that he was no longer a suspect.

Cecelia looked up, her face still drawn and anxious. She clearly didn't trust herself to speak.

"I think we must know a little more, Inspector," said John Allsworthy quietly. "Her parents are on their way here now . . ."

"One of the great difficulties that highly successful fraudsters have," began Sloan a trifle pedantically, "is concealing the proceeds of their crime."

"Money talks," observed Crosby to the world at large, "in more ways than one."

"When we looked for the signs of great wealth in the Bolsover and Durmast families we couldn't spot them," continued Sloan. "William Durmast and his daughter were living in just the style we would have expected, and although Bolsover and his wife both have very expensive hobbies . . ."

Cecelia looked up. "Oh?"

"He has a large heated greenhouse with exotic plants in it and she collects Bow china."

"I'd forgotten that."

"They nevertheless live in a house, if anything, rather rather smaller than their visible income warranted . . ."

"They've got a cottage in Provence as well," said Cecelia.

Sloan shook his head and said gently, "Not a cottage, Mrs. Allsworthy."

"Not a cottage?" She looked up.

"More like a château," said Crosby. "A socking big house and an estate to go with it. Vineyard and all."

Cecelia Allsworthy stared at the two policemen.

"Where in France?" asked her husband sharply.

"That was the trouble," said Sloan.

"St. Amand-sur-Nesque," said Crosby who had been practising its pronounciation.

"Did Hortense know him, then?" asked Cecelia uncertainly.

"Or did he know Hortense?" put in her husband swiftly.

"We're not sure," said Sloan, "but either way we think that Bolsover was afraid that she might recognise him and blow the gaff about his little country cottage in Provence."

Cecelia frowned. "Lucy did once say that neither she nor her father had ever been invited there. Because it was only one up and one down, the Bolsovers said."

"More like 'the House That Berry Built,'" said Sloan. The French police had acted with great celerity and he had the exact details at his finger-tips.

"Poor, poor Hortense," said Cecelia Allsworthy with a catch in her voice. "And I was the one who told him about my *au pair* girl being homesick for St. Amand-sur-Nesque." Dismay joined grief on her face. "When I joked about her going to sit in his hot-house . . ."

"We think," said Sloan gently, "that that's where the hyoscine came from—the hot-house, I mean. The conditions were just right for growing datura—one of the oldest poisons in the book."

"I understand all about the mode of poisoning, Sloan," said Superintendent Leeyes testily. "My next-door neighbour has one of those patches on his chest for his heart trouble. It saves him having to take his tablets all the time."

"A dermal delivery system," said Sloan, "is what the pharmaceutical people call it."

"And if Bolsover grew the plant, I take it that he could get at the poison?"

"Yes, sir." Sloan let this simplification of what must have been a very complicated chemical process pass. Its very nature, though, meant that Bolsover had had the possibility of murder in mind long enough to cultivate datura in his hot-house and make an extract from it—or would it have been a distillation? The forensic chemists would tell him all in good time.

"What I don't understand," said Leeyes with increasing vigour, "is why Bolsover had to kill Kenneth Carline in the first place?"

"Bolsover and Carline were both due at the Palshaw Tunnel at two o'clock on the Monday afternoon, sir, remember? To agree on the final handing over of the retention sum on the contract."

"Well?"

"On the Friday afternoon I reckon Carline comes in to see Bolsover and reveals that he had spotted a major discrepancy in the construction of the tunnel. It's the logical moment for him to have done so if you think about it."

"What discrepancy?" growled Leeyes.

"Bolsover," swept on Sloan, "probably says something like 'I expect there's some mistake somewhere but we can always check when we're over there on Monday. Come and see me on Monday morning and we'll talk about it.' And sends him off for the weekend."

"Does he indeed?" said Leeyes acidly.

"Carline goes off for the weekend and Bolsover gets to work. He arranges for Carline to get roughed up at the Rugby game . . ."

"Hrrrmph," grunted Leeyes.

"Which gives him the opportunity of taking a piece of plaster out of his first-aid kit cabinet and sticking it behind Carline's ear without arousing comment."

"Timed very nicely to work later, I suppose?"

"Oh yes. Bolsover is a very careful and clever man. He needed to be to accomplish fraud on the scale that he did."

"What I have been asking for some time," said Leeyes with heavy patience, "is what fraud exactly?"

"The Palshaw Tunnel," said Sloan impressively, "is precisely one metre narrower than it should be."

Leeyes stared at him.

"And I should have thought of it before," said Sloan, "because of something Harry Harpe said right at the very beginning."

"Harpe? From Traffic? What have Traffic Division got to do with it?"

"Don't you remember, sir, that Harry told us about two big lorries getting tangled together in there. We put it down to the drivers being foreign." Sloan slid over the point as quickly as he could: the superintendent's xenophobia started at the end of Dover pier.

"There wasn't as much room in the tunnel as there should have been? Is that what you mean?"

"I reckon that that was why they bumped into each other, sir."

"Someone must check on these things, Sloan."

"The County Surveyor's Department, sir." He paused. "That's where the fun begins."

"I'm waiting."

"There were two sets of plans for the Palshaw to Edsway Tunnel," said Sloan. "One for the design drawn up by William Durmast, who is generally thought of as a brilliant civil engineering architect. These plans are agreed by the County Council which have been appointed agents by the Department of Transport for the construction of the tunnel and the contract is put out for tender."

"Nothing wrong with that."

"Nothing, sir. William Durmast's plans are perfectly all right, the quantity surveyors do their job, a firm called Clopton's get the contract and the department approve and agree funding."

"Nothing wrong with that either." Leeyes was beginning to get peppery again.

"No. But afterwards a complete set of tunnel plans—and I do mean complete—are substituted by Ronald Bolsover in his office; by the County Surveyor at Shire Hall; and by the boss of Clopton's over in their headquarters. All long after Durmast has done his side of the work and started to get caught up in the designing of Mgongwala. He takes off for Dlasa and isn't really concerned with the tunnel detail any more."

"I have always said," declared Leeyes didactically, "that the bigger the fraud the easier it is to get away with."

"It was so simple that it probably didn't occur to anyone that it could have happened," said Sloan. "And if they did happen to check, they would have found that Durmast's, the designers and structural engineers; Clopton's, the contractors; and the County Surveyor's Department of the Calleshire County Council, the commissioning authority; were all working to the same plans and so would probably have thought the mistake was theirs."

"What about the Department of Transport?" asked Leeyes. "They're not fools." This wasn't the superintendent's usual view of them but today was different.

Sloan nodded his head. "I agree, sir, that that was the point of greatest risk because their plans were the originals with the proper width of tunnel on them. The width, incidentally," he added, "that they were helping to fund the County Council to build."

"It doesn't really matter, Sloan," grumbled Leeyes, "which way the government takes money of you. Rates and taxes all come to the same thing in the end. Don't you make any mistake about that."

"No, sir." Detective Inspector got back to the subject of the murder with all possible speed. Once started on the iniquities of government there would be no stopping the superintendent. "Because the department's interest was potentially dangerous, Bolsover staged a diversion on the day when there would be most officials about."

"The anti-nuclear protesters?"

"There was something very contrived about that demo, sir. It was one of the things that put me on to the nature of the fraud. Once you accept that someone wanted the tunnel portal covering up on the big day, you know where to begin to look. And it would have been child's play for Bolsover to put the leaflets in Carline's car," added Sloan. "He probably did that on the Monday morning before he set off for Lucy Durmast's."

"So it wasn't a sympathetic traitor within the gates who let the mob in after all?"

"It was Ronald Bolsover," said Sloan, "who opened the gate in the fence and left the key in the inside of the lock."

"And told the Wainwright woman that it would be open?" The superintendent blamed almost all forms of organised protest on the suffragettes. It was they, he insisted, who had made agitation a respectable occupation for respectable women.

"Yes, sir," said Sloan, hastily steering the conversation away from another hobby-horse. "Bolsover wanted them to lower their banner over the entrance and cause as much confusion as possible."

"They did that all right," said Leeyes warmly. "You should see Sergeant Watkinson's report."

"With the desired effect," said Sloan. "The press handout with all the dimensions was ignored by all the journalists and if anyone did check the photographs they would find the exact width was obscured by the banner."

"They couldn't get the Minister away quickly enough, I do know that," said Leeyes.

"The department had the County Council's certificate that all was well—which it was, according to the plans in Shire Hall. Besides, sir, where most frauds in tunnel building take place is in the skimping of the thickness of the tunnel walls."

"Make them thinner by even very little and you save a lot?" suggested Leeyes.

"Precisely," said Sloan, "but Clopton's didn't cheat there at all. The tunnel wall is as thick as the specification says it should be." He paused. "No, the beauty of it all was that all the people below the top three were working to the same plans . . ."

Leeyes grunted.

". . . and those plans were accurate in every respect except that the diameter of the tunnel was less than was being paid for."

Leeyes jerked his head. "Clopton's got paid for the bigger tunnel and split the extra three ways, I take it?"

"Yes, sir." He hesitated. "I know that's usually dangerous," he went on, his mind going back to one of Geoffrey Chaucer's *Canterbury Tales* "but it seems to have worked this time."

"How long is the tunnel?"

Sloan told him.

"And what does a tunnel smaller by one metre mean in money terms?"

"Ten percent of the materials element in the contract price."

"Good God, Sloan! Are you sure?"

That same gentle mathematics master who had painfully inculcated quadratic equations into Sloan's mind had dinned something in about *pi* and circumferential areas too. Enough for him to have been able to ask the right questions of a specialist. "Quite sure, sir."

"Even a three-way split of that is a lot of money."

"Yes, sir." Little wonder that Mrs. Eric Othen had worn a mink coat at the opening ceremony. The boss of Clopton's didn't need to conceal his wealth: it was expected of successful contractors.

"And where does the girl—Lucy Durmast—come into all this?"

"She doesn't, sir. Except perhaps as a suspect. Lucy Durmast only knew she hadn't killed Kenneth Carline. She didn't know who had and she didn't want to say anything until she knew who had."

"What can't speak, can't lie," said Leeyes Delphically.

"Nor did she want to say anything that might involve her father or compromise the building of Mgongwala."

Leeyes grunted.

"Another thing," said Sloan, "was that she didn't know if she was in danger, too. After all, she didn't even know why Kenneth Carline had been murdered—only that he had been."

"And what about her father?" Leeyes wanted to know. "Was he involved?"

Sloan shook his head. "William Durmast is the archetypal design man. He did the original plans—the ones that Bolsover got Carline to retrieve when he was at the Old Rectory—and then went off to fresh fields and pastures new. He's an inspired structural engineer and a great ideas man. Not a carrying-out-of-routine-work man. That's why he needed someone like Ronald Bolsover coming along behind him. Bolsover was a careful man."

"Esau was an hairy man," said the superintendent trenchantly, "and look where it got him."

"There was something I should have spotted early on," said Sloan. "Something that Cecelia Allsworthy said about a celebration party when the two ends of the tunnel met."

"What about it?"

"Bolsover wasn't in England at the time. He was in Provence. If anything had gone wrong at that point—and it was probably the most dangerous time—he wouldn't have been around to face the music."

"There's something else you should have spotted as well," said Leeyes loftily. "Something that should have immediately have aroused the deepest suspicions of any self-respecting investigating officer right from the very beginning."

"Sir?"

"The contract was on schedule."

His Honour Judge Eddington took his time about settling himself in his chair in the Crown Court in the county town of Calleford and consciously assumed the mien that customarily went with his mantle of office. His behaviour didn't quite fit Goethe's ideal of "without haste, without rest": true, there was no haste about his movements but he looked rested enough for an old man. There was in any case about him, too, the rather restrictive decorum—gravitas, perhaps, would have been a better way of putting it —that habitually went with overweight.

At last he indicated that he was prepared to begin.

He had, he reminded the Court, sentenced the accused to seven days' imprisonment for contempt of court and she was being brought before him at the end of that time . . .

A week, he refrained from reminding the Court, was a long time in law as well as in politics.

. . . having now, he trusted, purged that contempt.

The Clerk read out the charge. "How say you?"

"Not guilty," said Lucy Durmast. Her voice was low and pleasant. It was the first time that it had been heard by the Court. Her manner was commendably restrained but she looked like someone who had started to sleep again.

Cecelia and John Allsworthy were there, he in a dark suit with Regimental tie; she in grey with touches of mauve.

Prosecuting counsel rose to say that the Crown offered no evidence against the prisoner; indeed, that charges had been preferred against another person.

Judge Eddington considered the Court from his eminence and announced that he had a few words to say about *onus probandi*.

"What's that, sir?" whispered Detective Constable Crosby sotto voce into Sloan's ear.

"The burden of proof," went on the judge before Detective Inspector Sloan could speak, "is only assumed—nay, borne—by the Crown and you will not need me to tell you that it is a very real burden."

Lucy Durmast looked like Christian in *The Pilgrim's Progress* after his burden had slipped from his shoulders. Her hair positively shone.

"The accused," continued the judge, "rightly or wrongly—and it is not for me to say—chose to leave that burden where it lay." He coughed. "All I can say is that it can be a dangerous course of action which might be sound in theory but—ahem—perhaps a trifle risky in practice."

"He's dead right there," murmured Crosby not nearly inaudibly enough.

"Quiet," growled Sloan.

"And not to be commended as a general rule," said the Judge. "Over the centuries it has been established that by custom defence counsel do have a role to play even in the—er—clearest of cases."

"Jobs for the boys," said Crosby irreverently.

"I want," said Judge Eddington, "also to say something about judicial discretion. I must remind you all that this includes the right to be wrong. That we are all gathered here together today in the first place . . ."

"Now for the sermon," forecast Crosby.

". . . implies that there were two sides to the argument. There are always two sides to every case at law and two sides necessarily implies a choice." He paused. "A choice, I don't need to stress the Court, carries the inherent possibility of error."

"Here we go again," muttered Crosby.

"Were the law a certain animal," said Judge Eddington, "there would be no need for judges or judgements."

"Doesn't he know that it's an ass?" hissed Crosby.

Detective Inspector Sloan did not deign to reply. He merely gave thanks for the fact that they were sitting well back in the Court.

"It is also," continued His Honour, "one of the reasons why the right of appeal is very properly built into the judicial system . . ."

Into Detective Inspector Sloan's mind came a Spanish proverb that he had once heard and for some reason remembered. It ran "To every good judge, let there be a good action." The action in this case had all been elsewhere and most of it rather a long time ago now. Lucy Durmast hadn't ever really been part of it—just caught up in a nightmare. He wondered if she would be like Dreyfus and forgive if not forget.

"We must all be thankful," droned the judge, "that no serious miscarriage of justice has occurred . . ."

Lucy Durmast's eyes hadn't left Judge Eddington's face but her expression became very ironic indeed.

"Amen," said Crosby later as he and Detective Inspector Sloan left the Court.

There only remained the Epilogue.

"Where to, sir?" the constable asked as they walked towards their police car.

"Berebury," said Sloan. "But there's no hurry, is there, Crosby?" he added drily. "After all we've already had a trial run . . ."

Catherine Aird is a writer of Scottish descent who currently lives near Canterbury, England. She is the author of twelve previous novels, including *Harm's Way*, *Last Respects* and *Passing Strange*.